Hometown Family
Mia Ross

Love Inspired

Recycling programs
for this product may
not exist in your area.

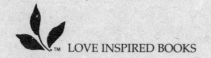

™ LOVE INSPIRED BOOKS

ISBN-13: 978-0-373-87744-7

HOMETOWN FAMILY

www.LoveInspiredBooks.com

Printed in U.S.A.

"After my mom died, it was really hard to be here. I left Harland the day after graduation."

Matt had never shared that with anyone, and he had no idea why he'd picked now to bare his soul. Caty put an arm partway around his shoulders, and he felt himself leaning into her.

He didn't know why, but just having her there made him feel slightly less miserable. When he realized he wasn't fighting it, he knew he'd gotten way too close to this sweet, understanding stranger.

Angry with himself for losing his grip, he pulled away and got to his feet. "I don't know why I told you all that."

"Told me what?" she responded lightly. "We're just out here, getting some fresh air."

Her smile promised she'd keep his emotional meltdown to herself, and he managed a halfhearted one of his own. "Thanks… You introduced yourself as Caitlin, but everyone calls you Caty. Which do you like better?"

She shrugged. "Whichever."

After studying her for a few seconds, he decided, "I like Caty. Suits you better."

MIA ROSS

loves great stories. She enjoys reading about fascinating people, long-ago times, and exotic places. But only for a little while, because her reality is pretty sweet. Married to her college sweetheart, she's the proud mom of two amazing kids, whose schedules keep her hopping. Busy as she is, she can't imagine trading her life for anyone else's—and she has a pretty good imagination. You can visit her online at www.miaross.com.

If you can believe, all things are possible.
—*Mark* 9:23

Dedication:

For Elaine

Acknowledgments:

First on this list is my editor, Melissa Endlich,
who generously took me under her wing
and made a place for me at Love Inspired Books.

Waving to all the wonderful folks at Seekerville
(www.seekerville.blogspot.com) who offer advice
when I need it and always make me smile.

Donna, you taught me how the law should work.
I hope you see some of yourself in Caty. Misty, no
matter what, you can always make me smile. Beth
and Elijah, you patiently listen to endless writer
talk and remind me how cute little boys are.

Most of all, I'm grateful to my family and friends
for hanging in there with me through the
tough times and celebrating the bright ones.
I couldn't have done this without you.

Chapter One

Caty McKenzie hated funerals.

As an attorney, she'd attended dozens of them, for personal and professional reasons, but she would never get used to them. Some were heart wrenching, others were just generally sad, but no matter the circumstances, she couldn't wait until the solemn ceremonies were over.

It was a two-hour drive from Charlotte, North Carolina, to her hometown. She pushed the speed limit most of the way and by the time she arrived in Harland, there wasn't a single parking space open near the church. Cars lined both sides of the street, and people were walking in from as far away as Main Street. She wedged her MG convertible into a spot reserved for motorcycles and hurried toward the oldest of the four churches that framed the town square. At the top of the steps, she found a hand-lettered sign tacked to the open door.

"Our little church is not large enough to hold everyone this morning. Please join us on the south lawn to honor our brother Ethan Sawyer."

She looked through the stained-glass window over the altar to see what must be more than two hundred people seated in chairs, on benches, some sitting on the ground or just standing. The outpouring of respect for Ethan made her throat swell, and her vision blurred with tears she didn't dare shed. Once she started, she wouldn't be able to stop. To get through this awful day, she had to be strong and composed. Later, when she was alone, she'd give in and cry her eyes out.

Caty went back down the steps and headed across the grass. It was a bright August morning, with sun streaming down through the leaves on the trees while birds circled overhead, chirping to each other. To her mind, the beautiful weather didn't match up with the congregation's somber clothing and muted conversation. Today they were burying one of her favorite people in the world. It should have been gloomy and dark, not cheerful and bright.

As she searched for a place to sit, she glanced toward the podium at the head of the makeshift aisle. Wearing his customary gray suit and paisley tie, Pastor Charles was talking to an incredibly tall, broad-shouldered man with dark, curly hair. He looked vaguely familiar, and she actually did a double take.

Matt Sawyer.

Caty hadn't seen him in, what? Ten years? Fifteen? She was in junior high when he had graduated from high school and left without a backward glance, off to adventures she could only imagine. Not that it mattered. Even back then, he probably couldn't have picked her out of a three-person lineup. A North Carolina all-state linebacker four years running, in high school he was good-looking, self-assured and cocky. She'd admired him in a general way, but they had never been friends. You couldn't be friends with someone who didn't even know you existed.

Judging by his stiff posture, he was uncomfortable being here, and she couldn't recall ever seeing him in church with his family. Caty didn't realize she was staring until his gaze swung her way. It wasn't her memory of her teenage years playing tricks on her—he really did have the bluest eyes she'd ever seen. Accented by the determined set of his jaw, today those eyes were filled with misery. Caty knew she'd looked much the same at her grandfather's funeral three years ago. No matter how long one had been away, it was always heartbreaking to come home to say goodbye to a loved one.

At a loss, she sent him a sympathetic look. All she got in return was a puzzled frown before he joined his family. One of his sisters leaned in and said something to him, but he scowled and shook his head. Undeterred, she said something else. His warning glare got through to her, and she gave up, facing forward with an exasperated sigh.

Calling for their attention, Pastor Charles addressed the crowd with arms outstretched. "If you'll all take your seats, we'll begin."

Caty found an empty seat near the back and perched on the very edge of the bench. Aunts, uncles and cousins of the Sawyers clustered around them, lending support on what must have been a horrible day for them. Pastor Charles, bless his heart, announced that he'd keep things short due to the warm day. For Ethan's children and grandkids, the brief ceremony was a godsend.

"And now, let us pray." When everyone had bowed their heads, he continued. "Merciful Father, hear our prayers and comfort the Sawyer family in their time of need. Renew our trust in Your Son, whom You raised from the dead. Strengthen our faith that Ethan Sawyer, who died in the love of Christ, will share in His resurrection and live with You, now and forever. Amen."

Silently, Caty added her own prayer for Ethan's family. The aftermath of her grandfather's death was still clear in her memory, and she knew they'd need all the good wishes they could get.

Matt and his younger brother, John, stepped forward to take the lead positions to carry their father's casket out to the waiting hearse. John was clearly struggling to keep his composure, and Matt gave him a look of encouragement as they made their solemn way through the assembly. In response, John straightened and nodded back.

Caty had no idea how they endured that emotionally charged walk. Glancing up, she got the distinct feeling that Ethan was watching them with incredible pride. After the hearse door closed, the funeral director began organizing everyone for the trip out to the cemetery. Caty headed for her car, only to find it corralled tightly between a Cadillac and an enormous black SUV.

"Blocked in?"

She turned to find Matt behind her and tried to laugh it off. "The top's down, so maybe I can just climb in without opening the doors."

He gave her a quick once-over, from her white blouse and slim black skirt, straight down to her four-inch black heels. Her "funeral uniform," it got more use than she liked. The skirt fell way below her knees, but for some reason his quick appraisal still made her blush.

"Not very likely." Now he gave her car the same assessing look. "Nice MG. What year is it?"

"A '68." From the way he'd asked the question, she could tell she didn't look familiar to him. "You have no idea who I am, do you?"

He really shouldn't admit it, Matt cautioned himself. Ladies liked to think they were unforgettable, and he always obliged. So he took a minute to study her. The longer he looked, the better he liked the view. She wasn't model material, but the sunlight picked up strands of red in her brown hair, set off by fair skin and the dark green of her eyes. Looking closer, he noticed the freckles sprinkled across her nose. Totally at odds with her classy outfit, they made him think of summertime, but he still couldn't place her.

Finally, he admitted defeat and shook his head. "Sorry."

"At least you're honest." She held out her hand. "Caitlin McKenzie."

As he shook her hand, he rolled the name around in his mind a few times but still came up blank. That probably meant he hadn't met her recently, so he took a shot. "From Harland."

He'd meant to make it a statement, stalling for time until he could place her. Instead it came out as a question, and he cringed at how lame he sounded. Then again, he'd already botched their little reunion so badly, he figured it didn't matter much.

"John and I were friends growing up," she explained patiently. "We graduated together."

"So you're a few years younger than me." Even as he said it, he knew it sounded as though he was dragging his feet in this conversation. Which, of course, he was.

Suddenly, something far back in his memory clicked. "I remember Hank and Martha McKenzie."

"My grandparents."

"And a quiet little girl with glasses." Considering how confident and classy she looked today, he had a hard time connecting her to that mousy kid. "That was you?"

"A long time ago."

Reaching into his pocket, he pulled out his key fob and pressed the button. Across the parking lot, a dark blue pickup chirped in response. "You can ride with me if you want."

As a limo pulled into line behind the hearse, she asked, "You're not going with your family?"

He shrugged. "Not enough room for all of us."

She gave him a doubtful look, but fortunately she didn't press. "Okay. Thanks."

When they got to his truck, he opened the passenger door for her. "Thanks for coming today."

"I'm glad to do it. I just wish it wasn't necessary," she said as she climbed into the truck.

Standing inside the open door, he looked in at her. Her response sounded so polished, he knew she'd rehearsed it many times. "You've said that about a thousand times, haven't you?"

"I guess so," she admitted with a frown. "I'm sorry if I sounded like a robot. I just never know what else to say."

"Yeah," he murmured, staring at the hearse as it slowly left the lot. "Me, neither."

As Matt settled into the driver's seat, he finally placed her. "Caty Lee McKenzie. Valedictorian, right?"

She didn't exactly smile, but it was closer to a grin than anything he'd gotten since she had introduced herself. "Right."

Trying to salvage the conversation, he added, "Guess we didn't run in the same circles at school."

"I wasn't a cheerleader." Her smile evaporated, and she gave him a chilly look before turning to stare out the window.

She really knew how to hurt a guy. Then again, he thought as he put his truck in gear, he'd never really been into brainy women. They were way too much work.

After the mercifully brief graveside service, the long parade of cars headed through town to the Sawyer farm. As they drove along Main Street, well-kept houses stretched out on either side. Alongside the pavement were the original cobblestones, flanked by a canopy of oaks that dated back to the Civil War. In Harland, gardens were immaculate, porches were welcoming and the sweet tea was always fresh. Even though she'd left to realize her dream of becoming a lawyer, Caty had always been drawn back to the place that had made her who she was.

"I'm sorry for the reason, but it's good to be home again," Caty told him with a smile. "Someday I want to come back for good. How 'bout you?"

"I plan to stay as far from Harland as I can get."

The certainty in his voice startled her, but she plowed ahead. "So, where are you living these days?"

"Charlotte."

"Really? Me, too." As of yesterday, that wasn't technically true anymore, but she didn't think he really cared that much. "How long have you been there?"

"A few months now," he answered without taking his eyes off the road.

He didn't elaborate, and she tried again. "I haven't seen you since high school. What have you been up to?"

"I'm a mechanic."

Oh, he was a real talker, this guy. "Whereabouts?"

"California, Arizona, Texas. Spent about a month in Michigan. Way too cold."

She realized he'd answered her questions without revealing a single personal detail. He'd done it artfully, as if he'd had a lot of practice. Fortunately, her legal training had made her adept at worming information out of reluctant people.

"Do you like Charlotte?"

"Yeah." Just when she thought he'd leave it at that, he added, "My boss hired me to work on classics at his body shop, which is great. I love old cars."

Progress, she congratulated herself with a little smile. "How did you get into that?"

"Got certified for regular work, then started playing around with some clunkers at the shop I worked at in Houston. When I was done, the owner sold 'em for more than he spent on the wrecks. He cut me in on the profits, so I did some more. When I decided to move back to North Carolina, he called a friend of his and gave me a reference."

She hoped to keep him talking by giving him a harmless compliment. "That takes a lot of skill. You must make good money."

He slanted her a look she could only define as suspicious. "I do fine."

Okay, so money was a bad subject. Caty switched back to classic cars.

"I love my MG, but I know next to nothing about it. If I get in and it starts, I'm happy. Come to think of it, it was making a weird clunky noise when I pulled in at the church earlier."

"I can look at it if you want," Matt offered as they pulled off the main road onto a lane marked Sawyer Farm.

"I didn't mean to hint for free help with my car," she explained. "I'm happy to pay your regular rates."

"No problem, sweetheart."

Matt drove past the rambling white farmhouse and parked beside several cars in the turnaround in front of one of the barns. He shut off the engine and came around to open her door. The truck sat high enough that she could look him dead in the eye.

Making full use of the higher ground, she gave him her most intimidating lawyer's glare. "*Do not* call me that."

He gave her the most clueless look she'd ever seen. "Why not?"

"Guys like you use cute nicknames to cover up the fact

that you can't remember the names of all the women you date, that's why. Baby, honey, doll, things like that." She ticked them off on her fingers, grimacing in disgust. "It's insulting."

Shaking his head, he offered his hand to help her down. "Whatever you say, Caitlin."

Batting his hand away, she climbed out on her own. "That doesn't count. I told you my name half an hour ago, and we're not dating."

"Got that right," he muttered.

The two of them stalked off in different directions, and Caty wondered if he was as glad to be rid of her as she was of him. She'd tried everything she knew to be pleasant, but he wasn't having any of it. The man was hopeless.

The black Lab snoozing on the back porch lifted his head as she approached. When he recognized her, he thumped his tail in welcome.

"Hey, Tucker," she said softly, scratching underneath the stars-and-stripes bandanna tied around his neck. "How're things here?"

Brows furrowed in that Lab way, he cocked his head and whined. "I know," she sympathized. "But don't worry. It'll be okay."

He answered with a couple more tail thumps, then settled his chin on his paws as she stepped over him to knock on the back door. When a familiar voice yelled for her to come in, Caty smiled and went inside.

All the windows were open, and whirring fans drew fresh air through the house. There were four women in the kitchen, one spooning batter into muffin tins, another emptying the dishwasher. The other two were arguing over how much coffee to put in Marianne's commercial-grade double-pot coffeemaker.

With her graying hair and slender build, a casual observer would think the smaller one was at a disadvantage. Anyone who knew her knew she hadn't lost an argument since she was old enough to talk. A longtime widow with eight grown sons and grandkids numbering in the twenties, Ruth Benton had the courage of a lion. And the heart of a pussycat.

"Ruthy, I should've known you'd be here."

The field general of the little army dropped her point midsentence and turned to her with a delighted smile. "Caty Lee McKenzie, is that you?"

"Yes, ma'am."

Ruthy rushed over to fold her into a hug, then grasped her arms and pushed her away to look her up and down.

"Too skinny," she chided, pressing her lips into a disapproving line. "What? They don't have decent restaurants in Charlotte?"

"None as good as yours."

"You could learn how to cook." Ruthy took a pair of ruffled red oven mitts from the counter and pulled them on. "It's not that hard."

"Not for you ladies, anyway." Caty included the others with a smile, then focused back on their leader. "The tables outside are full of food. What's all this?"

Ruthy moved a wire rack to a clear spot on the counter. "Those kids will have enough to do without worrying about what they're going to eat the next couple days."

Caty looked around and laughed. "Couple days? I think they're set for the week."

"It's not much." Harland's favorite chef waved off the compliment with her spatula, using it to transfer one of the yummy-looking pastries to the cooling rack. "Just a little of this and that."

From the side porch, Caty heard voices and the sound of a filling washing machine. "Are they doing laundry?"

"Sure are. There's a mountain of it back there, some clean, some not. I set two of John's darlings on it. Told them they could each keep a pair of his boxers for their trouble."

Caty grinned. "He doesn't wear boxers."

"They don't know that," Ruthy replied, the laugh lines around her eyes crinkling as she winked. She shoved a tin of her famous blueberry muffins into the oven and turned to Caty with a suspicious look. "And how do *you* know that?"

"Truth or dare, junior year."

The older woman studied her long and hard, then chuckled and shook her head. "If you ask me, a man's old enough to live on his own, he's old enough to do his own laundry."

"Marianne likes taking care of him. Besides, his house is about a hundred yards away."

"Still, he could come up here and take care of it himself. She's got enough to do, what with teaching and taking care of her kids and this big house. I don't know how Ethan got by without her all those years."

"He didn't eat as well, that's for sure," Caty agreed, sneaking a piece of flaky crust that had fallen on the counter.

Ruthy saw her do it but just smiled. "I always thought you and John would get together."

Actually, he'd asked. Many times. Caty adored him, and tempting as it was, she had no intention of joining his endless collection of admirers. "Why ruin a good friendship?"

"All the time you were in college, you never brought a beau home. I know you had them, but did you bring them to meet me? Not once."

"I didn't want you to go stealing them away from me," Caty replied with a grin.

She *hmphed* at that. "More likely you had that nose of yours buried in your books. You always did."

"That's what it takes to be successful."

Ruthy pinned her with a knowing look, and Caty got the distinct impression that those wise blue eyes could see right through her. These days, she was accustomed to dealing with acquaintances, people who respected her but didn't really know her. Sometimes she thought Ruthy knew her better than she knew herself.

"You're way too serious, sweet pea. If you want to help, I've got plenty of big pans that need washing."

"Yes, ma'am."

Caty stepped out of her gorgeous but very impractical shoes and set them on the mat by the back door. Then she rolled up her sleeves, tied on an oversize apron and started scrubbing.

Chapter Two

Feeling very out of sorts, Matt took a couple deep breaths to calm his temper. He wasn't easy to rile, but the very classy Caitlin McKenzie had gotten under his skin in record time. Maybe it was the intelligence driving her sharp tongue. Or the way she had looked at him with more sympathy than he deserved. After his nasty parting shot, he figured he wouldn't get any more of that from her. It was his own fault, but he regretted starting out so badly with her.

Then again, he thought as he approached his family, that was the least of his problems.

His younger sister Marianne saw him first, and he couldn't miss the annoyance she quickly tried to mask with the smile she usually reserved for company.

"Kyle," she said, "why don't you and Emily go in the kitchen and get a snack?"

"Sure, Mom." He spun his little sister around and headed her in the right direction. "C'mon, Emmy. Grown-ups wanna talk."

As they walked away, Matt was struck by how much taller his nephew had gotten. Eight years old, Kyle had a longer stride than Emily's, but he slowed down to match her smaller steps. *Responsible* was the word that came to mind. He had to be, since his father had taken off four years ago, just after Emily was born, leaving Marianne to fend for herself.

"The kids were great during the funeral," Matt said when he realized they were all waiting for him to say something.

"Thanks," Marianne replied in the clipped, polite voice she probably used on telemarketers. "So were you."

"You sound surprised."

"I was."

"You've been on my back since I got here," Matt shot back. "I came as fast as I could."

"Maybe if we'd had your new phone number, we could have reached you in time to..." Her voice trailed off, and tears started gathering in her eyes. With a frustrated sigh, she said, "I think I'll go see if Ruthy needs help finding anything."

As she walked away, John plunked a hand on Matt's shoulder. "Don't mind her. Losing Dad this way has been real tough on her and the kids."

"It's more like she still hasn't forgiven me for leaving home fifteen years ago," Matt complained.

"Actually, she understood that. It's the never coming back she has a problem with."

"I was back for Christmas."

"Not last Christmas."

"I told you." When he realized how loud his voice was, Matt notched it down. "My boss booked a lodge in Telluride and one of his friends cancelled. I've always wanted to go, and all it cost me was a plane ticket."

John didn't respond to that. His disgusted look said it all.

"What do you want from me?" Matt demanded. He had

nothing to apologize for, and he didn't like being made to feel otherwise.

"I don't know," John shot back, eyes narrowing to icy blue slits. "Maybe for you to visit 'cause you want to, instead of feeling like you *have* to. Now that you're in Charlotte, it's not that far. Caty manages to get here every few weeks."

"I have a life, y'know."

Swooping in from the side, his baby sister, Lisa, wedged herself in between them, snaking her arms around them.

"We all have lives," she reminded them in her peacemaker tone. "But right now, we have to stick together."

That got their attention, and they let the pointless argument drop. They'd replayed it a hundred times at least, and Matt suspected John was as tired of it as he was.

When the porch door opened, they all glanced over to see Caty coming down the steps. Wearing an apron way too big for her, she set down on a nearby table the tray of finger sandwiches she was carrying. She'd ditched the fancy shoes, Matt noticed. Her bare feet made an interesting contrast with the buttoned-up skirt and blouse she was wearing. He wondered how her hair would look down around her shoulders, curling around those sparkling green eyes.

Get a grip, he warned himself sternly. She was very far removed from the kind of women he usually spent his time with. Then there was the whip in her voice when she basically scolded him for being male. It stung more than it should have, and he knew better than to ignore it.

Now, though, she was all warmth and caring as she hugged John and put a comforting arm around Lisa. "How are you two holding up?"

"Okay, I guess," Lisa answered. "I didn't get to talk to you earlier, but I was so happy to see you at the service."

"Ethan was one of my favorite people. If he hadn't organized that scholarship fund for me, I'd be drowning in student loans instead of just wading."

"Ever since you were little, he knew you'd do something important when you grew up," Lisa reminded her. "Dad just figured he was helping things along. He said, with you as his lawyer, he'd never have to worry about legal stuff again."

"He convinced a lot of people in Harland to contribute money so I could afford to go to Boston College." She paused with a fond smile. "It was an investment, he told them. When they needed a lawyer, they'd know one they could trust. Most of them couldn't afford it, but they gave anyway. I'll never forget it."

That sounded like his father, Matt thought with more than a little pride. His dad had a knack for seeing things in people that even they didn't know were there. If he'd seen it in Caty all those years ago, there must be something to it.

"Did Ruthy put you to work?" John asked as Caty removed her apron.

"Just a little. How's Gina doing?"

"Fine," he answered smoothly. "I think she's seeing that plumber who just moved to town."

"When I was here last, she was seeing you."

He shrugged. "Things change."

"There've been at least two since her." Lisa ratted him out. "And those are only the ones *I* know about."

"No promises, no hard feelings," John said with a grin. "Right, Matt?"

"Don't drag me into this," he protested, raising his hands. "I don't know where you learned that stuff."

"From you," Lisa informed him curtly. "Leading by example."

"Anyway," Caty said, "I'll be in town awhile. If there's anything you need, just let me know."

Her interpretation made Matt wonder if she was trying to protect him from another tongue-lashing. Considering the way she'd reamed him out, it would be pretty sporting of her.

"Tomorrow's Friday," Lisa reminded her. "Don't you need to get back to work?"

For some reason, Caty hesitated before saying, "I decided it was time for a visit."

While she chatted with John and Lisa, Matt was only half listening. There was more to her extended stay, but she clearly intended to keep it to herself. Matt knew all the classic signs, and there was no missing them. She was obviously close to his family, and he'd quickly learned she wasn't shy about speaking her mind.

Whatever she was hiding, it must be serious. He barely knew her, but the thought of the pretty lawyer being in trouble really bothered him.

Around six o'clock, the last of the relatives left and the house was empty. After all the activity, the quiet rang with a sad finality. Caty was packing the last of the dishes into Ruthy's catering carts when the Sawyers came into the kitchen.

"I just can't believe it." Sinking into a chair, Lisa stared down the table at the head seat where Ethan usually sat. "He's gone."

As she dissolved into tears, Marianne sat beside her and put an arm around her shoulders. "It'll be okay, Lise. We'll be fine."

"No, we won't," Lisa sobbed. "We won't ever be fine again."

Patting her back, Marianne glanced at the far counter,

which was still stacked with containers of food. "What in the world?"

"Ruthy," Caty answered, handing over a handwritten note.

"'The fridge is full, coffee's ready to go,'" Marianne read out loud. "'Warming instructions on everything. If you need me, call anytime. All my prayers tonight are for you kids. God bless you all.'"

Lisa sniffled, dabbing her eyes with a tissue.

Matt opened his mouth, but Marianne cut him off with a stern look and a quick shake of her head. Grimacing, he crossed the kitchen to get a glass from the cupboard and fill it with water. As he stood with his back to them and stared out the window, Caty noticed the stiffness in his broad shoulders.

At least his brother and sisters had said goodbye to Ethan. Matt would never have that chance. How on earth would he get past that?

Not that it was any of her business, she cautioned herself. He was a grown man, and he made his own decisions. Why he'd chosen to neglect his family was none of her concern. She wasn't in a position to advise him and, even if she were, he probably wouldn't listen. Only a fool intruded where she wasn't wanted. Which reminded her, she really didn't belong here right now.

"Marianne, could I borrow your van to go into town? They're holding a room for me at the B and B."

"Don't be silly." Standing, Marianne turned on the flame under a teakettle labeled Full. "You can stay here. We all are."

"Matt's staying with John, and the sofa bed in the living room is comfy," Lisa added as she thumbed through a basket of tea bags on the table. "I'll be in our old room with Marianne, so you're welcome to it."

"It's been a long day, Caty." John took the seat across from hers and opened a jar filled with Ruthy's famous oatmeal cookies. "You've been running around helping with everything, on top of that long drive. Just stay here and relax."

Only one Sawyer hadn't invited her to stay, and the silence stretched awkwardly as they all stared at Matt's back. He didn't seem to notice.

"Matt, is it okay with you if I stay?"

"Sure," he answered without turning around. "It's not my house."

"It is now." Marianne pinned Caty with a hard look. "Isn't it?"

"We'll go through all that later," she hedged.

"We'll go through some of it now." Handing Lisa a steaming mug, Marianne sat down with her own. "I know Dad redid everything about a year ago, and since you were his lawyer, I assume you helped him do it. Next week, I'm supposed to start prepping my room for my new class. Kyle starts school the week after and Emily's registered for pre-K. If we need to move, I have to know. Now."

Caty hesitated. There were good reasons for not releasing estate details so soon. Emotions were too raw, and people needed time to deal with their loss before they got practical. Another reason was that if they got caught up in the provisions in the will, they put off grieving, sometimes with very serious consequences.

There were steps in the process, and it was best to go through them in the order dictated by psychologists who were experts in the field. In a psych class, Caty had learned about Dr. Elisabeth Kübler-Ross, who put the stages of grief into a nice, neat list: denial, anger, bargaining, depression and acceptance. The Sawyers were still in denial.

Intellectually, Caty knew they should go through the others before she told them anything.

Then she thought of Ethan, how deeply he loved his family. He wouldn't want Marianne and her kids worrying about where they were going to live.

She began by giving Marianne a reassuring smile. "I can tell you all the buildings and land within three acres of the main house are yours. Provided you let John live in the carriage house as long as he wants."

Marianne visibly relaxed. "Thanks, Caty. I should've known Dad would do it that way."

"What else can you tell us?" Lisa asked.

They'd finally gotten Matt's attention. He didn't join them at the table, but he'd turned and at least appeared to be listening.

"We're all here," Marianne added. "And I'm sure you know the important things. Why not handle it now?"

Pushing aside her misgivings, Caty relented because she knew it was what her client would want. "Ethan's major assets were his life insurance and the farm, which goes to the four of you. Whatever you do with it has to be a unanimous decision."

Matt moved to the island and leaned in, looking like a drowning man who'd found a rock to cling to. With his bitter comment about staying away from Harland so fresh in her memory, she suspected that was exactly how he felt.

"You mean we can sell the farm?" he asked.

Caty circled the table with a somber look. "Provided you all agree, yes."

"Well, I don't want to." John crossed his arms stubbornly, glaring at nobody in particular.

"There's two thousand acres here," Lisa chided.

"Twenty-two hundred and four," he corrected her.

"With the price of land these days, it must be worth a

fortune," she continued. "You can't knee jerk such a big decision."

"I'll buy you out then," he insisted, looking to Caty for support. "I can do that, right?"

He looked so hopeful, she didn't have the heart to remind him he didn't have nearly the amount of money that would take. "If the others agree, yes."

Marianne was toying with her spoon with a pensive expression. "If we keep the farm, who's going to run it?"

"I will," John volunteered. "I know every inch of this place, and all the guys like me."

"Which is why they never listen to you," she responded. "You're one of the Indians, not a chief."

"Dad must have had someone in mind," Lisa said with a puzzled expression. "But who?"

Caty's gaze landed squarely on Matt, and he thought his heart thudded to a stop for a few seconds.

When it started up again, he bit back a curse, because in his mind this was still his father's house. Standing on the other side of the island, he was outside the circle at the table. Suddenly, it felt much too close.

"Not a chance," he growled. "I'm not moving back here."

"Matt, be reasonable," Marianne said in that because-I'm-the-mom voice every kid hated. "Someone has to run this place, and Dad chose you."

"We'll hire a foreman."

She gave him a doubtful look. "In the middle of harvest season?"

"You can do that," Caty explained. "Ethan paid himself a salary, and proceeds from the life insurance can be combined with that to hire extra help. After twelve months, whatever insurance money is left goes equally to John, Lisa and Matt, and into trusts he set up for Kyle and Emily."

"I'll just take it out of my portion," Matt offered. It would be worth every penny to keep his sanity.

Frowning, Caty shook her head. "It doesn't work that way. Any remaining funds will be divided equally among the five of you."

Matt barely stifled a groan. Without much in the way of living expenses, he could step in and run the farm for almost nothing. Hiring someone on such short notice wasn't impossible, but the price was bound to be astronomical. If he chose to do it anyway, he'd be stealing money from the others. His father knew him well enough to be confident Matt would never do that.

While he searched for some kind of compromise, he stalled for time. "How much are we talking here?"

For the first time, Caty looked uncomfortable with the conversation. They'd put her in a tough spot, he suddenly realized, asking her to be professional while they sat around their kitchen table nibbling on leftovers. He could almost see the wheels spinning in her head while she shuffled through information only she knew. After a long silence, she finally answered.

"Half a million."

Marianne gasped something incoherent, and Lisa squeaked, "Dollars?"

"Yes."

John didn't say a word. Rocking back in his chair, he stared across the kitchen at Matt, waiting.

The invisible noose was back, crushing Matt's throat until he could barely breathe. They all expected him to backtrack and embrace the life he'd escaped fifteen years ago. Sure, he could do it, but it would drive him crazy, getting up at dawn every day for fourteen hours of back-breaking work that could all be wiped out by a single hailstorm.

He was not, and never had been, a farmer, rooted to the ground he walked on, worrying about blight and insects. Watching the sky and hoping for rain, watching the rain and hoping for sun. Just thinking about it made his skin crawl.

The last eyes he connected with were Caty's, and he finally found what he was looking for. Sympathy.

"This is a lot to consider," she said in a firm, gentle voice he was convinced could soothe a rushing bull. "For now, I think it's best if you just focus on finishing out the harvest. There's plenty of time for the rest."

"I guess you're right," Marianne agreed, dishing up some potato salad before passing it to Lisa. "The kids and I have a lot to do, getting ready for school."

As the conversation began spinning around the new topic, Matt mouthed Caty a thank-you. She gave him an encouraging smile, and the invisible band crushing his chest loosened just enough for him to breathe again.

"I'll go pull your van in, Mare." Without waiting for an answer, he grabbed her keys from their hook and strode out the side door.

Parking the van took all of a minute, but he wasn't near ready to go back inside. It had been a long day of fighting against his emotions and biting his tongue to keep from upsetting his family. Deciding he needed some time to himself, he wandered through the backyard and over to the pond. He walked out to the end of the dock and sat down, letting out a long, frustrated sigh.

He was now one-fourth owner of a farm he didn't want, had never wanted. At least the house was Marianne's. He couldn't stand living here for very long, but he knew he could never bring himself to sell the Sawyer homestead.

It would have broken his father's heart, and even though he was gone, Matt couldn't bear the thought of letting him down. Again.

He heard a door slam, followed by the light footsteps of someone a lot smaller than John. His sisters would know better than to follow him out here, so it must have been Caty. As he scooped up a handful of gravel, he had to admit her sarcastic cheerleader comment had impressed him. In a classy, no-nonsense way, she'd put him firmly in his place.

She wasn't like the other women he knew, he mused as he tossed a pebble into the water. Then again, none of them had a serious job like hers. None of them would have been at a funeral on a beautiful summer day when they could have been playing hooky from work at a lake somewhere. Lobbing in another stone, he watched the ripples work their way through the water.

"Hey, there." Caty offered him something wrapped in a napkin. "I thought you might be hungry."

Another stone plunked into the water. "Not really, but thanks."

Anybody else would get the hint that he wanted to be left alone. But not this one. She actually came closer.

"It's kind of warm inside. Do you mind if I hang out here for a few minutes?"

Matt shrugged. "Suit yourself."

"Thanks."

She sat a couple of feet away, not too close but close enough that he couldn't forget she was there. He also couldn't miss the subtle scent of roses that had come with her. Light and sweet, it suited her perfectly.

Man, he was tired. Turning into a regular poet. He waited for her to say something so he could tell her he really wasn't up for company. To his surprise, she remained totally silent. Leaning back on her hands, she looked up at the sky while she wiggled her toes in the water.

For a long time they sat there side by side, not even looking at each other. Matt continued tossing pebbles, and Caty seemed content admiring the surrounding fields. Frogs croaked around them, intent on being louder than the crickets, and a couple of ducks glided past, eyeing him warily. They reminded him that this was their place, and he was only visiting.

That didn't do much for his mood, and he whipped the last few pieces of gravel into the water. None landed near the ducks, but they didn't appreciate the noise and quickly changed course.

With his hands empty, Matt eyed the muffin still sitting on the dock. Deciding that he didn't care if she thought he was an idiot, he picked it up and broke off a piece. He popped it in his mouth and sighed in appreciation. "Blueberry's my favorite."

"I'm glad."

She still wasn't looking at him. He knew because he kept glancing over, and he didn't catch her eyes even once. This was a new one for him, since women usually connected with him pretty fast.

"Want some?" he asked, holding out the muffin.

"Sure. Thanks."

As he handed her half, her eyes finally met his, and he was struck by the directness of her gaze. He dwarfed her and hadn't exactly been friendly, but she didn't seem the least bit intimidated by him. The cute suit had some guts. Who'd have figured on that?

They munched in silence for a few minutes, and Matt tore the napkin in half to share with her.

"Thanks." After wiping her mouth and hands, she stood up. "I'll leave you be now."

Her bare feet rustled through the grass as she walked away from the pond. She was a few yards away when he heard himself call out her name.

She turned, and a shaft of late sunlight hit her like a spotlight. If he were superstitious, he'd think someone was trying to tell him something. He shook off the weird feeling and went on. "You mind hanging out awhile longer?"

She took a step toward him and stopped. "You're sure?"

"Yeah."

She hadn't pushed him to talk, hadn't tried to be entertaining or lift his spirits. She'd just let him sit there and stare at the water. It made him wonder if somehow she understood how he felt.

When she sat back down, he realized it was getting cool and her pretty blouse wasn't much for warmth. He pulled off his jacket and draped it across her shoulders.

"Thanks."

"No problem." Sighing, he stared at the house he'd avoided like the plague for so many years. "I wish I could've said goodbye."

"You're not just talking about Ethan, are you?"

Her perceptiveness was unnerving, to say the least. Avoiding her eyes, he stayed fixed on the house and shook his head. Then, for some insane reason, instead of leaving it there he started to explain.

"When I was ten, our mom got real sick. I didn't know it then, but she had leukemia. She went to the hospital and didn't come home. We had supper with her one night and the next morning she was gone. I never got to say goodbye."

Caty put a sympathetic hand on his shoulder. He hated it when women tried to baby him, but for some reason her gentle touch didn't bother him.

"That's so sad. You must have missed her so much."

"Marianne was seven, but John and Lisa were too young to understand. Lisa doesn't even remember her." His voice broke, and he cleared his throat. Even after all these years, talking about it was almost impossible.

Folding his hands in an effort to control his emotions, he stared down at them. "After she died, everything changed."

He expected Caty to jump in and finish his thought, maybe fill in the blanks for him, but she didn't. To his surprise, her patient silence actually made him want to keep talking. Hands clamped into helpless fists, he lifted his head and met those bright green eyes.

"The older I got, the harder it was to be here. I left Harland the day after graduation. Dad said he hated to see me go, but he understood. No matter what I did, he always said he understood, but I'm not sure he meant it."

Matt had never shared that with anyone, and he had no idea why he'd picked now to bare his soul. Too tired, he figured, to keep his mouth shut.

"He loved you," Caty said, rubbing his shoulder. "He wanted you to be happy. If that meant leaving home, he was okay with it."

Matt wasn't so sure about that, but he didn't have the energy to argue with her. From leading his careless lifestyle to ignoring his family, he knew he'd disappointed his father too many times to count. Now it was too late to fix what he'd broken.

Tears stung his eyes, and he held them back with the heels of his hands. Caty put an arm partway around his shoulders, and he felt himself leaning into her. He didn't know why, but just having her there made him feel slightly less miserable. The warmth of her went beyond the physical, drawing him in. When he realized he wasn't fighting it, he knew he'd gotten way too close to this sweet, understanding stranger.

Angry with himself for losing his grip, he pulled away and got to his feet. "I don't know why I told you all that."

"Told me what?" she responded lightly. "We're just out here getting some fresh air."

Her smile promised she'd keep his emotional meltdown to herself, and he managed a halfhearted smile of his own. "Thanks."

"No problem."

He went a few steps, then turned back. "You introduced yourself as Caitlin, but everyone calls you Caty. Which do you like better?"

She shrugged. "Whichever. I'm not picky."

After studying her for a few seconds, he decided, "I like Caty. Suits you better."

Matt turned and headed for the house, leaving Caty there, wondering what on earth had just happened. While she'd also lost her own mother at a young age, hers had simply vanished from her life. Lost in an accident with a coworker who'd had a few too many drinks after work. Caty couldn't imagine how difficult it would be for a child to watch a parent wither away from illness. Matt had been old enough to know what was happening but too young to accept that she was gone.

Always missing her, wishing she could come back. Tears welled in Caty's eyes as she pictured that little boy growing into a young man, bitter and furious, desperate to leave those painful memories behind. But Ethan had still been there, along with John and the girls. The pull of the farm fought with Matt's need to be somewhere else. Anywhere else.

Judging by Marianne's coolness toward him, his solution had only created more problems for his family. Over the years, he'd probably decided it was easier to stay away than come home and face the music. Unfortunately, it had kept him from being there when they needed him, and he could never change that.

Guilt is a terrible burden to carry around, no matter how strong you are.

Chapter Three

After spending the night on the Sawyers' couch, Caty woke as the sun started peeking through the living room's sheer curtains. She was usually up before now, but her long day had completely knocked her out.

She folded the light blanket and stowed it with her pillow in a hand-carved chest. After a couple of tries, she managed to fold up the sofa bed and replace the cushions and throw pillows. Stepping back, she decided everything was the way Marianne had left it and glanced into the antique mirror next to the front door.

Dressed in one of John's battered football jerseys and a pair of Marianne's capris, she wouldn't win any beauty contests, but she was more or less presentable. She caught her hair up in the clip she'd worn yesterday and padded into the kitchen to start the coffeemaker. While it gurgled, she saw Tucker sitting on the back porch, gazing in longingly through the screen door. He had free run of the entire farm, but apparently he was feeling lonely.

"Morning, boy," she greeted him, holding the door open. "Want to come in?"

Panting, he thumped his tail with enthusiasm and looked

over his shoulder toward the field road that wound alongside the woods.

"You want some company?"

The thumping increased, and he spun a couple of tight circles before settling back on his haunches with an expectant look.

"Okay." She laughed. "Give me a second."

Most of the cups were too small to hold her usual dose of morning coffee, so she ended up with a huge purple mug sporting "Lisa" in fancy silver script. The dot over the *i* was a star, and the mug played "When You Wish Upon a Star" when she poured in her coffee.

"Totally Lisa," Caty commented to no one in particular as she spooned in creamer and sugar. After a quick taste, she decided it worked and headed out the back way with Tucker.

He bounded down the lane toward the restored carriage house John called home. When Tucker raced up the steps and did some more spinning, Caty noticed Matt in a chair on the little porch. The Lab ducked his head under Matt's hand, delighted with the ear scratching he got in return. Ten seconds of that was enough, and he repeated his come-with-me dance for Matt.

"Looks like you've snagged a partner already, boy," he said with a guarded look at Caty.

She'd thought they were starting to become friends, so it was tough not to take his attitude personally. Reminding herself that he needed some understanding, she bit her tongue and forced a smile. "Tucker's motto is The More, the Merrier."

There, she thought. She wasn't exactly asking him to come along, but she'd made it clear she didn't mind if he took the dog up on his wagging invitation. Matt didn't move at first, but eventually he got to his feet.

"I'd hate to disappoint you," he told Tucker, avoiding her completely. The dog bolted from the porch and galloped up the road, glancing back to make sure they were following.

Matt's long strides quickly took him past her, and when he got to the top of the small hill, he stopped to look over at a gnarled old oak a few yards away. The impassive look on his face changed, and she got a glimpse of the same grief she'd witnessed last night. Out of respect, she stopped, too. He seemed to be wrestling with something, and she didn't want to intrude. To her surprise, he turned to her with a pensive expression.

"This is—was—Dad's favorite place on the farm." He glanced out over the hill toward the wheat fields becoming gold as the sun rose behind them. "He had all that, and he liked this old tree more than the rest of it."

Caty took that as an invitation to come closer, and she paused a few feet away. Judging by Matt's anguished memories of his own past, she suspected that, while he respected Ethan's fondness for the old tree, he didn't share it.

"Y'know," he said with a scowl, "you're really easy to talk to."

The warm blue of his eyes took some of the sting out of his comment, and she smiled. "You make that sound like a bad thing."

"It usually is. For me, anyway."

She wasn't sure what to make of that, so she decided to ignore it. "Want some?" she asked, offering the mug.

When he hesitated, she thought he'd refuse, but he took it from her. "Thanks." He swallowed some coffee with obvious difficulty and pushed the mug back at her as if it held something poisonous. "What's in that? Frosting and whipped cream?"

"Creamer and sugar," she answered, taking a sip to prove it wasn't nearly as bad as he made it out to be.

"Any coffee at all?"

"Sure. At the bottom," she added with a smile.

He looked as if he hadn't slept a wink all night, and she was hoping to lift his spirits with some humor. Not that it should matter, considering the way he'd treated her. The problem was that it just wasn't in her nature to stand by and let someone suffer. Her supervising partner had knocked her for that very thing on her last performance appraisal. He'd called it "excessive sympathy." She called it being human.

Shaking his head, Matt gave her a flicker of the lopsided grin she remembered from high school. "Lemme guess. You're one of those hot-fudge-sundae-in-my-coffee types."

"Mmm, sounds perfect. Don't tell me. You're one of those high-test, straight-up caffeine types."

"Most men are."

"I know lots of guys who like gourmet coffee," the lawyer in her had to argue.

"Your boyfriend likes it that way?"

"I don't have one." She had no intention of telling anyone in Harland about David. She'd left him—and those awful memories—behind in Boston. That was exactly how she wanted things to stay.

Matt grinned at her. "Why am I not surprised?"

"Because you're a cynic who can't see beyond Friday night."

"At least I enjoy Friday night," he returned evenly. "I'm not chained to a desk somewhere waiting for my life to start."

Appalled by the very personal attack, Caty didn't know what to say. She glared up at him, but he deflected it with an I'm-smarter-than-you-think-I-am look.

"Go ahead," he goaded. "Say it."

"Not in a million years."

"Okay," he conceded with a chuckle. "But I know what you're thinking. It's written all over that pretty face of yours."

She knew he was baiting her, but she wasn't a trout. Inwardly seething, she cautioned herself against getting too close to this guy. He might not realize it, but he was now her client. That meant she had to be friendly but professional.

Tucker doubled back and ran circles around them, flopping on the ground so Matt could give him a belly rub.

"I'm real sorry I didn't remember you," he said while he scratched behind the Lab's ears.

The quiet apology cooled her temper, and she decided to give him a break. "That's okay. I was pretty forgettable back then. Invisible, more like."

Matt glanced over his shoulder. "Not anymore."

Feeling her cheeks start to burn, she turned away, pretending to watch Tucker bound back into the tall grass. "So this was Ethan's favorite place. Why?"

"We'd have lunch here sometimes, him and John and me," he explained. "Y'know, like they used to in the old days. We'd eat and talk, mostly about nothing."

"That sounds nice."

"It was."

Matt seemed so distant from his family, Caty was amazed to learn how much he valued that simple memory. She'd have thought he'd do his best to forget everything connected to Harland. It was nice to discover she was wrong.

In his next breath, all semblance of nicety vanished.

"But I have my own life now." Stepping closer, he glowered down at her. "Did you and Dad consider that when you boxed me into this little trap?"

Caty recognized that he was trying to intimidate her, use his size and considerable muscle to make her give in. She couldn't miss the shift in his phrasing, dropping the responsibility for his predicament squarely on her shoulders. Fortunately, she had a weapon or two he hadn't counted on, and she brought them out now.

She stepped closer, shrinking the distance between them to show she wasn't afraid of him. Well, maybe she was a little, but she could fake it.

"Don't get testy with me, Sawyer. I'm on your side."

He opened his mouth, but she narrowed her eyes and cut him off with a warning look. Fortunately, he paid attention and settled for a disgusted sigh. It was insulting, but she let it go.

Pushing down her own frustration, she focused on the pain she knew he was feeling and softened her expression just a bit. "I'm trying to be patient with all of you. You've had a terrible shock, and I understand that. I'll do my best to take some of the burden off you, but I can't make it go away completely. The law works the way it does to protect everything Ethan worked so hard for. You have to be patient with me, too."

That wasn't what he'd wanted to hear, and he planted his hands on his hips like a petulant child, looking anywhere but at her. *Quit being such a baby,* she wanted to say, but she held back. It wouldn't go over well.

When he did meet her eyes, she saw something she hadn't expected. Fear. So quietly she almost didn't hear, he said, "I don't know what to do."

Her heart tripped over the raw emotion in those few words, and she swallowed hard against the sudden lump in her throat. Hoping she appeared calm and dependable, she willed her most professional tone into her voice. "I know. I'll help you all I can."

The thought of working so closely with Matt didn't thrill her, but she simply couldn't leave him with the accordion envelope and letter of instructions that she gave most of her clients. Once the immediate crisis of bringing in the harvest was over, he'd have some big-time decisions to make.

Balancing his own wishes against the obligation he felt to his family simply wasn't possible. He could put it off awhile, but eventually he'd have to choose between them. Someone was going to be incredibly disappointed.

After their little powwow, Matt and Caty headed inside for breakfast. As they came through the door, John and Lisa were already at the table and Marianne was dishing up some of the biggest omelets he'd ever seen.

"Where are the kids?" Matt asked, hoping they might give him a reprieve from the discussion he'd been dreading since Caty had outlined his father's plans.

"The Millers invited them over to play, so I let them go," Marianne replied as she set their plates on the table and sat down. "I thought we could use the time to talk things over."

Perfect. Barely stifling a groan, he pulled out a chair for Caty and sat down next to her.

Marianne poured them both some coffee and set the pot on a cork pad.

"So, Matt," she began. "How long are you planning to stay?"

The careless tone was completely fake, intended to throw him off his stride. Over the years she'd perfected it, and he'd felt himself tense up as soon as she opened her mouth.

Something nudged his boot underneath the kitchen

table, and he glanced to his right to find Caty giving him the eye. She lifted her glass of orange juice and while she sipped, she shook her head just enough that he couldn't miss it. He reminded himself they were all exhausted and more than a little on edge, trying to deal with something that had blindsided them all.

Matt wasn't used to considering other people when he made his decisions, so this was an uncomfortable stretch for him. Hoping he looked reasonably calm and not scared to death, he looked at each of them in turn. "I haven't decided yet. First I want y'all to tell me what you need from me."

At a rare loss for words, his sisters traded confused looks. For the first time he could remember, he knew how they felt.

"Nothing," John assured him. "You've got a life to get back to, and you should go. I'll figure something out."

Lisa started to protest, but he silenced her with an uncharacteristically harsh look. She glared back before stabbing a fork into her untouched breakfast. She didn't say anything else, though. Marianne was completely silent.

Oddly enough, his family's unwillingness to ask Matt to stay was what made up his mind.

"Okay, here's the plan." When he had their attention, Matt continued. "I'll stay through the fall to get things squared away here. Make sure all the crops get in, do a total maintenance round of the equipment, stuff like that. Beginning of November, we'll sit down again and see how things look."

"What about your job?" Lisa asked. "And your apartment?"

"It's only three months, so I'm not worried about the rent." That wasn't entirely true, but right now it was the least of his concerns. "I'll talk to my boss and see what he can do. If he can't hold a spot for me, I'll find another one."

"Jobs are hard to come by these days," Marianne reminded him.

"Thanks for the news flash."

His sarcasm got him a saucy look. "I just meant that if things don't work out in Charlotte, you'll have a job here."

There was no way he was returning to Harland permanently. The compromise he was proposing would take him dangerously close to the edge of his limit. He'd go nuts if there was no end to his stint as a full-time farmer.

Now wasn't the time to dig in his heels, though. They'd all have to cooperate to finish out the harvest season. "My boss knows what's going on, but for this I want to talk to him in person. At some point, I'll go back to Charlotte to see him and pack."

"When?" Marianne asked.

"When I can," Matt replied evenly. "I know flexibility isn't your favorite thing, but if this is gonna work, you have to cut me some slack."

"And you have to give me something to work with," she retorted. "I can't keep this farm and our family on track if you're going to just do your own thing all the time."

The rigidity rubbed him the wrong way, but she did have a point. "I'll do my best," he promised.

"We all will," John added, and Lisa nodded enthusiastically.

Relieved at the fairly easy agreement they'd come to, Matt dug into his omelet. Loaded with diced ham and cheddar cheese, it was the scallions that gave away the chef. "Ruthy was here, I see."

"She brought a huge basket of food just a little while ago," Marianne answered. "I told her it really wasn't necessary, but she insisted her boys couldn't work all day without a proper breakfast."

"I love that woman," Lisa said around a mouthful of cranberry muffin.

"Too bad she can't teach you to cook," John teased. "Then maybe somebody'd wanna marry you."

"Plenty of guys want to marry me," she informed him haughtily. "I just don't want to marry them."

"Y'know, there are no knights in shining armor anymore," he said, only half joking.

"There's still one around somewhere," Lisa shot back. "I'll find him eventually."

"Good luck, darlin'."

"Women don't like nicknames like that," Matt informed him, carefully avoiding Caty's gaze. "Makes 'em think you can't remember their name."

Lisa pinned him with a suspicious glare. "You do it all the time."

"Not anymore. I've been reformed."

"By who?" she demanded.

In between bites, he nodded at Caty. "She straightened me out yesterday. Imagine, all these years I've been doin' it wrong."

John laughed, and Caty sighed. "Sorry, girls. I tried."

"Takes a brave lady to tell Matt anything," John said, still chuckling.

"No lack of guts in this one, that's for sure," Matt agreed. For some reason, the conversation came to a grinding halt. They could almost hear the squeal of brakes, and Matt flashed a look around the table. "What?"

"Nothing," Lisa replied quickly, pouring herself some more juice.

Silence seldom reigned in the Sawyer kitchen, but it settled like a weird haze over the normally lively table. Caty jumped in to fill the awkward silence. "Matt, could I ask you a huge favor?"

"Shoot."

"Could you drop me in town so I can pick up my car and get my stuff?"

"Sure."

He pushed back his chair to stand, but when Marianne cleared her throat he reluctantly sank back down. He knew what was coming.

"We have some tough days coming up," she said, looking at each of them in turn. "We're going to need every bit of strength from everyone in this family to get through them, but I think we all know that won't be enough."

She took Lisa's hand on one side and Caty's on the other. John reached out for his brother's hand, and Matt swallowed a groan. "Marianne—"

"You don't have to believe, but the rest of us do," she informed him haughtily, her nose actually tilted in the air a little. "As part of this family, I'm asking you to just sit there and keep your mouth shut for thirty seconds."

In response, Matt folded his hands and rested them on the table in front of him. The others bowed their heads, and he forced himself to stay in his seat. He hated this kind of thing, but out of respect for them he kept quiet. If they needed this, he wouldn't ruin it for them by reminding them that God had very selective hearing.

"Lord," Marianne began, "please bless our family with the patience and courage we'll need to weather this storm. Guide us with Your wisdom and help us do what's best for all of us. And please," she added in a quivering voice, "tell our parents we love them."

As John and Lisa added their own sentiments, a small hand settled over his and gave a little squeeze. Caty hadn't lifted her head, but he appreciated the kind gesture. Her hand was a distinct contrast to his own. Dainty and polished, it looked vulnerable next to his much larger one.

Then again, he'd learned there was nothing vulnerable about Caty McKenzie. In her own way, she was just as tough as he was. She didn't back down when she probably should, and she did everything she could for people who needed her. Even when they didn't deserve it.

When he'd all but begged for her help, he'd fully expected some kind of runaround about it not being her job. Or she wouldn't have time, or some other excuse. When she'd agreed, a huge weight had lifted from his shoulders, and he'd felt that he could breathe again. There was something about her. More than sympathy, more than kindness, it was something he couldn't quite define. Then it hit him.

He trusted her.

Wary by nature, it usually took him a long time to trust people, but Caty had earned his confidence in just a few short hours. By refusing to let him push her away, she'd proven she would stand firm when things got hard. That kind of attitude probably came in handy when you dealt with other people's problems all day long.

He figured it also made her a real handful, which explained why she was single. No man in his right mind would get tangled up with a woman like her. Still, after so many years of relying only on himself, it was nice to know the spunky lawyer had his back.

"Amen," Marianne finished, the others echoing her in hushed voices.

Matt unfolded his hands to find them white from clenching so hard. He rubbed them together and stood. "Ready when you are, Caty."

He was halfway out the door when Marianne called his name. Braced for a scolding, he turned back. "What?"

She gave him a smile so rare, he'd forgotten what it looked like. "Thank you."

Some of the frost between them melted, and he returned the smile. "You're welcome."

When she heard the rock music coming from Matt's truck stereo, Caty asked to change the station.

"Go ahead," he replied. "I don't really hear it anyway."

She scanned until she found a popular local morning show, and he groaned. "You like country?"

"I like all kinds of music recorded in this century."

"Perfect."

"You said you don't hear it," she reminded him sweetly. "Would you like me to switch it back?"

"No, it's fine."

He did the male version of an eye roll, and she muted a laugh into a smile. When they got to the town square, she had to laugh. "My car looks kind of ridiculous, parked in the middle of nothing like that."

"Just a little," he agreed with a faint smile.

Before she could unlock the door, he came around to open it for her. These days, old-fashioned manners were hard to come by, and she'd gotten used to fending for herself. She had to admit, Matt's chivalrous streak was pretty appealing. As if being darkly handsome and built like an oak tree wasn't enough, she groused silently.

After she got out, he appraised her MG with an appreciative whistle. "This is one gorgeous car. How'd you get it?"

"My grandfather found it in a junkyard and towed it home with the parts in boxes. He restored it for me as a gift for finishing law school. He died a month later." Her voice wavered, and she stopped talking. Her life had gone on, but it was still hard to face losing him.

"So it's more than a set of wheels to you," Matt said gently.

"A lot more."

"Yeah, I get that. Never knew a woman that did, though." Then he gave her a knowing look. "So…what's the big secret?"

Her heart thudded to a stop. He lived in Charlotte, so it was possible he'd heard about it. Maybe some obscure article had shown up in the newspaper or online. The thought of it made her stomach turn. Falling back on her legal training, she counted to three and stalled.

"I'm not sure what you're talking about."

"I hope you're better in court than you are at lying."

"I'm a fabulous lawyer! An *honest* one," she added with venom.

He didn't react one tiny bit, and she blew out an exasperated breath. "You're mean."

"I've been called worse, believe me." His eyes had gone a murky bluish-gray that could only mean trouble. "You don't want to tell me, fine. But I know something's wrong."

Caty looked down at her gold MG key ring, rolling it around in her hand while she debated. When she met his eyes, she saw something that surprised her: concern. Matt was worried about her. She couldn't imagine why he cared, but if she kept quiet, he'd only worry more. With everything else going on, that was the last thing he needed.

"You trusted me, didn't you?" she asked.

He nodded. "I promise to keep it to myself."

It hadn't occurred to her that he wouldn't, which shocked her. People had to work hard to earn her trust, but he'd already done it, without her even noticing.

"Okay, but not here." She nervously glanced around to see if anyone was watching them.

His frown deepened into a scowl. "How bad is it?"

"Bad enough that I don't want the entire town to know, at least not just yet. Do you remember where my grandparents' house is?"

"Oak Street. I'll follow you."

Traffic had hit its usual midmorning lull, and they made it across town in no time. She parked in the cracked driveway, and Matt pulled in behind her.

As he got out of his truck, he stared at the house with a skeptical look. "How long's this place been empty?"

"Three years," she replied as she took a suitcase out of the tiny trunk. "I was living in Boston when Grandpa died. After the funeral, I just locked the door."

"Boston," he echoed in disgust. "Only use for all that snow is skiing, if you ask me."

"I'm with you on that one."

"Took you long enough to agree with me on something," he grumbled.

"We Scots are genetically stubborn."

He chuckled. "Is that *we* like 'us,' or *wee* like 'small'?"

"So clever. You should buy a microphone and do standup."

"Nah. John's the funny one."

She'd always thought so, but she was discovering that Matt had a wry sense of humor all his own. A little more subtle, but it was there if you were paying attention. A pleasant surprise, it made Matt seem more down-to-earth. When she put her key in the front door, she got a not-so-pleasant surprise.

It didn't work.

Caty pulled out the old brass key and checked the color of its little plastic frame. Green, for home. It was the right one, so she inserted it again and added some elbow grease. The tumblers squealed but finally rotated with a very rusty click.

"Needs some WD-40," Matt said. "I'm sure there's plenty of other stuff around here that could use it, too. Might want to start a list."

Making a face at him, she pushed the door open. "I'll remember."

Dusty was the first word that came to mind when she stepped inside. *Musty* was a close second, along with *dark.* The last were easy enough to fix. Two of the cracked shades ripped when she tried to raise them, and the dirty windows muted the sunlight. As she took a good look around, she thought maybe keeping things dim wasn't such a bad idea.

"Looks like the set for a haunted-house movie, doesn't it?" she asked, her voice echoing around the living room. Dust-covered sheets were draped over everything and busy spiders had fashioned cobwebs into creepy swags hanging from the ceiling and the corners of every doorway.

Everything was still where Grandpa had left it, right down to the salt and pepper shakers on the rack above the stove. With no one around to wind it, the grandfather clock in the hallway had stopped ticking long ago. Gram's prized Queen Anne sofa still reigned in front of the picture window, and her heirloom china filled the hutch along the far wall. It was as if time had stopped, trapping the little house in the past.

It should have depressed her, but it actually did the opposite. After so many years away, searching for a place that felt like home, she'd found it right here where it had always been.

"Well, it's looked better," Caty joked, turning to find Matt still standing in the doorway. "Come on in."

He came in a few steps and stomped his foot, unleashing the scurrying of furry feet. "Those are only the ones out in the open. There's no telling how many more of 'em there are."

"Afraid of mice?" she asked sweetly.

That got him. He joined her inside and folded his arms with a let's-get-on-with-this look.

"Okay." Nobody in Harland knew what had happened, and she wasn't thrilled about fessing up. Taking a deep breath, she let the words out in a rush.

"I got fired."

He didn't parrot the words back at her the way most people would have. Instead, he asked, "Why?"

"You heard me mention that scholarship fund your dad set up for me." Matt nodded, and she continued. "I keep a list of all the people who contributed, and whenever they needed legal help, I logged it in at the firm as client development. I came to Harland on weekends or vacations, did everything on my own time."

"No one at your office knew?"

She shook her head. "Pro bono work was allowed only for approved clients and charities. If my supervising partner knew about my work down here, he'd pitch a fit. So I didn't tell him."

"But he found out."

"He summoned me to his throne room this past Sunday morning and confronted me with a stack of papers. He claims he handles personnel issues on Sundays to avoid disrupting business, but I think it's a power play to ruin people's weekends."

She heard the bitterness in her tone and sent up a quick prayer for patience. "Anyway, he didn't have any actual proof because I did all that work at home with my own equipment and supplies. But he tripped me up like one of those moronic witnesses on TV. I decided to come clean and offered to make amends, but he wouldn't hear any of it."

"Nice guy."

"Tell me about it. He told me I'd gotten too close to my clients, and it clouded my judgment where the firm was concerned."

"Meaning you were too nice to us poor folk, and the bigwigs lost money."

"Basically."

She didn't mention that he'd threatened to turn her in for more official disciplinary action. Even though she wasn't sure it was a real possibility, just the thought of it scared her to death. She'd worked too long and too hard to risk destroying her career. While her instincts had told her to fight, she'd backed down and slunk out of his office before things got worse.

"Anyway," she continued, "he and his wife had brunch plans, so he gave me one hour to clear out my office and leave. Then he had the nerve to check through all my boxes, take my key and lock the front door behind me. By Tuesday, I decided the best thing was to come home, and I started packing. I was renting a furnished town house, so mostly it's books and clothes."

Matt looked well-and-truly amazed. "You did that all by yourself?"

"I'm perfectly capable of— What's so funny?"

He was grinning at her and shaking his head, for what was probably the tenth time since they'd met yesterday. She couldn't determine whether she was truly that baffling or if the gesture was actually aimed at himself. It didn't take a genius to figure out she wasn't the kind of woman he was used to hanging out with.

"Nothing." After a quick look around, he said, "But you can't stay here. It's a mess."

She bristled at his assessment of her house. Sure, it needed some TLC, but he made it sound as if it was ready for the wrecking ball. "It's fine."

"Oh, yeah?" He stomped his foot again and got the same scurrying response.

"I'll have Frank Hastings come out tomorrow to set some traps and block up the holes they're coming through." She mimicked brushing dirt off her hands. "Problem solved."

"You've got no electricity," he argued. "The well pump won't run without it, which means you've got no water."

"Today I will, Saturday at the latest. This is Harland, so they'll just flip a switch down at the substation. It doesn't take days, like in Charlotte."

"Do you even own a toolbox?"

"No, but I can buy one. And tools to go in it," she added before he could zing her.

"Will you know what to do with 'em?"

Now she recognized that he was teasing, and she took it in stride. "I'm not exactly the handy type, but they have lots of DIY stuff online. If I really get in a jam, I'll call Gus over at the hardware store. He'll help out."

After a few more tries, he finally gave up. "You're set on doing this?"

"Yes, I am."

Caty rolled up the sheet that covered the camel-back sofa. Stepping back, she admired its graceful lines with a fond smile.

"I remember sitting here in front of the fireplace with Gram, learning how to read. We traveled all over the world, had all kinds of adventures. I haven't had much time to read lately. When my books get here, I'm going to fix that."

"Sounds nice," Matt commented without a hint of teasing.

"I've been gone a long time," she murmured. "It's good to be home."

"I know, but until the electric's on, you're welcome to eat and shower out at the farm."

Considering the stuttering nature of their still-raw friendship, his concern for her was really sweet. "That I'll do. Thanks, Matt."

"No problem."

Following her lead, he grabbed the opposite end of the sheet that had covered her grandfather's rolltop desk and helped her fold it. Staring down at the desk, he let out a low whistle. He'd done that with her car, too, she recalled with a grin. Apparently, that was his customary stamp of approval.

"That's mahogany. Did your grandfather make this?"

"Yes," she answered proudly. "It took him two years, and he said he loved every minute of it."

"How come you didn't take it with you?"

Smiling, she ran a hand over the fluted cover. "For one thing, it weighs a ton. Mostly I thought it belonged here, with everything else," she added, looking around the room. Neglected for so long, it would take some serious work to get everything back to Gram's standards. But right now, time was something she had plenty of.

With the worst of the dust caught in the sheets, she figured it was okay to open the windows. She unlocked one but it wouldn't budge. Chuckling, Matt stepped in and wrestled the stubborn sash loose. It groaned in protest but finally rose, letting in a welcome breeze, scented with the honeysuckle running wild in the overgrown garden.

While he forced the rest of the windows open, she retrieved a dusty old broom and twirled it through the heaviest cobwebs. Fortunately, she'd had the foresight to roll up the enormous Oriental rug and leave it along one of the walls. Once she had swept the plank floor, she'd unroll the carpet and the place would look more presentable.

After chasing dust bunnies for a few minutes, she realized it was a losing battle. Taking her phone from her back pocket, she opened the notepad app and wrote down "test vacuum cleaner" and "WD-40."

When Caty and Matt couldn't quit sneezing, she called a time-out. They went on the front porch, and Matt strolled to his truck. He brought back two bottles of water and offered her one. "I've got a cooler in the console, so they're cold."

"Oh, thank you!" Taking a long swallow, she added, "Perfect."

He sat on the step below her, which put them almost eye to eye. For a while, they sat in companionable silence, enjoying the fresh air.

"Can I ask you something kinda personal?" he asked.

After all the help he'd given her today, she was feeling generous. "Shoot."

"How did you end up here with your grandparents?"

"Gram and Grandpa took me in when my mom died."

That got his attention. He rested one elbow over the step behind him, angling to look at her. "Really? How old were you?"

"Nine. She died in a car crash."

Of all the people she'd ever known, only Matt could understand how drastically that single moment had changed her life. Sympathy flooded his eyes, and he frowned. "I'm sorry."

"It was a long time ago," she said, hoping to lighten his suddenly somber mood. Parents dying was a hard enough subject any day, but for him right now it was even more so.

"I'm still sorry. What about your dad?"

"I never met him," she confided in a careless tone she

didn't feel. "Gram told me more than once we were better off without him."

"Did you ever try to find him?"

Very few people knew her history, so no one had ever asked her that question. Old wounds she'd thought long healed cracked open with an unwelcome jolt of pain. "He didn't want me. Why would I try to find him?"

Matt's face took on a pensive expression. "Did he know about you?"

"I don't know," she snapped. "We didn't talk about him. Ever."

"Then how do you know he didn't want you?"

"He left and didn't come back. What else was I supposed to think?" She swallowed hard to force down the emotions clogging her throat. She'd gone her whole life without him and had done just fine. It shouldn't hurt anymore, but sometimes it hit her unexpectedly and all she could do was ride it out.

Matt held up his hands in surrender. "Okay. I didn't mean to pry."

"I should let you go," she said, eager to let the topic rest. "I have a lot to do, and you need to get home."

"Charlotte is home."

She was in no mood to debate with him, and she rolled her eyes in frustration. "To the farm, then. Your family's waiting on you, I'm sure."

"Right." With a grimace, he got up and headed for his truck. At the end of the patchy stone walkway, he turned back. "You're still coming out later?"

The look on his face reminded her of Tucker when he thought you might not stop to pet him. After putting up with Matt's characteristic swagger, the momentary vulnerability made her smile.

Holding out her arms, she said, "Do I have a choice?"

His uncertainty gave way to that crooked grin. As much as she hated to admit it, it did have a certain charm.

"Guess not," he said. "See you later, then."

Chapter Four

Now that she had her car, Caty picked up some cleaning supplies and headed home. She worked for as long as she could, but when the dust got to be too much for her, she took a break. Sitting on her front porch steps with a bottle of lukewarm water, she wished she had an in-car cooler like Matt's. Her phone rang, and she was thrilled to see the exterminator's number on the caller ID. Fortunately, Frank was in town and promised to make her his next stop. She was just about to call the electric company when she heard footsteps turn onto her broken stone path.

Glancing up, she saw one of her neighbors out walking a wiry gray schnauzer. Prim and proper as her owner, the pooch sported a wide blue ribbon like the kind dressed-up children wore a hundred years ago. "Good morning, Mrs. Fairman. How are you today?"

"Sitting up and taking nourishment," the slender woman answered in a bold voice that belonged in a much larger person. With snowy white hair and the immaculate speech of a true Southern lady, Priscilla Fairman had been president of the Harland Ladies' League for Caty's entire life. She was also a constantly moving cog in the town's gossip mill.

"I'm glad to hear that." Caty patted the step beside her. "I don't have chairs yet, but would you and Annabelle like to sit awhile?"

"Thank you, dear. We'd enjoy a little rest."

Caty steadied her while she sat. Once she was settled, her guest said, "Forgive my poor manners, but I couldn't help seeing what you've been up to over here. Are you selling your house?"

"Not a chance," Caty told her with a smile. "I'm coming home."

Mrs. Fairman's face lit up as if it was Christmas morning. "How wonderful! It will be so nice having you here again. Young people aren't much for visiting these days, but you always make time for me."

"That's because I enjoy it so much." Careful not to squeeze too hard, Caty hugged her around the shoulders. "Tell me what's been going on lately."

"First I want to ask how the Sawyers are doing. George and I started our morning prayers with them."

"They're managing," Caty replied.

"That's good to hear. Such a horrible shock, Ethan going that way."

"Yes, it was."

Half expecting Mrs. Fairman to ask about Matt being here, Caty was relieved when the conversation moved on to less personal things. While her neighbor got her caught up on the goings-on around town, several more people stopped to wish them a good morning. A few even beeped, waving out their car windows on their way into town.

When Frank arrived, he greeted Caty with a bear hug and a demand that she come by for supper with his family sometime soon.

As he went inside, Mrs. Fairman wished her a pleasant day and continued down the sidewalk, with Annabelle trotting alongside. Waving after them, Caty called up an online phone book and dialed the power company. Frank's brother Alan answered.

"I heard you were back," he said with a chuckle. "What took you so long to call?"

"It's been a busy morning. I'm hoping you can get my electricity turned on sometime soon."

"How does this afternoon sound?"

"Perfect. Thanks, Alan."

"No problem. Welcome home."

Caty couldn't have asked for a better start to her day. Taking it as confirmation that she'd made the right decision, she looked up with a grateful smile. "Thank You for bringing me home."

After a few more minutes of lounging, she finished her water and went back inside. After partly unrolling the colorful Oriental rug, she discovered it now resembled very expensive Swiss cheese. There was nothing she could do about that, so she went into the back hallway and opened the case on the grandfather clock. It took a while to clean out the dust and get the movement freed up, but she patiently kept at it.

Once the pendulum was swinging freely, the steady tick-tock resonated through the empty hallway. With that memory restored, Caty felt more as though she was home to stay.

"Hello?"

A now-familiar voice called out from the front door, and she rounded the corner to find Matt standing in her living room with a small cooler in his hand. Looking around, he lifted a skeptical eyebrow. "How's it goin'?"

"Fine. Frank's getting rid of my furry guests, and the electric's going on this afternoon. How about you?"

"You want the 'fine' or the truth?"

She laughed. "The truth. I can take it."

"I'm hunting down our missing farmhands. Four of them didn't show, so I went by the apartment they were sharing. It's empty. No note, nothing."

As if things weren't bad enough for the Sawyers, Caty thought. Trying to sound positive, she said, "If they're that unreliable, you're better off without them."

"I guess."

"Does anybody know where they went?"

"Nope. If they're lucky, I won't find out."

He was still holding the cooler, and she asked, "Is that for me?"

"Since your fridge isn't working yet, I figured you could use some lunch."

Recognizing the hole in his account, she grinned. "I thought you were hunting for missing farmhands."

For a second, he seemed to be concocting a story. Fortunately, he didn't insult her with a lie. "Guess it was both."

Deciding not to make a thing of it, she took the cooler from him. "Well, thank you. I wasn't looking forward to PowerBars and warm water."

"You're welcome. Speaking of water, you know it's gonna be a mess when you turn it on, right?"

"Yeah," she replied with a sigh. "I'll run it for a while until it clears."

"Could take a couple days." When he noticed the rug, he groaned. "Whoa. That's not good."

"It's my own fault," she scolded herself. "I'm a country girl. I should have had the sense to mouseproof everything before I left. Of course, if I hadn't stayed at that cute B and B whenever I visited, I'd have known what was going on here. I guess I just assumed it would always stay the same."

"Yeah," Matt commented quietly, "I know what you mean."

Misery swirled through his eyes, and Caty's heart went out to him. If she'd known him better, she'd have given him a hug or said something profound to let him know she understood. Before she could come up with something appropriate, he withdrew and headed for the door.

"Matt?"

He turned, and she gave him her most encouraging smile. "It will get better, I promise."

"When?"

"When you're ready to let him go."

Grimacing, he shook his head. "Right now, I can't imagine that ever happening."

With that, he strode from her house, the screen door slamming behind him.

They'd been busy while he was gone.

Marianne, who had to be the most ruthlessly organized woman on the planet, was in charge of all things administrative for the farm. That included a computer database of suppliers, customers and the Sawyers' extensive Christmas-card list. The pile of condolence cards and emails on her desk had to be a foot high. Right beside them were two neat stacks of thank-you notes, stamped and ready to be mailed.

As soon as he walked through the door, Matt felt the anvil settle back on his shoulders. Equal parts responsibility and guilt, it was heavy even for him. "Looks like you've got everything under control."

"Lisa and John helped."

Matt scowled at her. "Meaning I haven't."

"Meaning nothing. It wasn't a dig, I promise."

Feeling foolish, he mumbled, "Sorry."

Being in Harland always put him on edge, but it would be unbearable if he didn't get hold of his temper.

As a start, he said, "When I called I forgot to tell you I invited Caty to come out for supper. Hope that's okay."

"Of course it is," she assured him as they walked into the kitchen. "Ruthy left us enough food for a month. This morning I found six casseroles in the freezer on the porch."

"Coffee?" he asked as he opened a cupboard for some mugs.

"Please."

After filling them, he set the cups on the kitchen table and took the chair opposite Marianne. When his father was alive, Matt had often sat at the head of the table without a second thought. Now you couldn't pay him to sit there.

"I know you're not supposed to tell a lady she looks tired."

"But I do," she acknowledged with a faint smile. "I know."

He wasn't sure what to say next. Then Caty's comforting words popped into his head. "It'll get better, Mare. How's everybody else doing?"

"All right, I think. Ruthy told Lisa to take some time off, but she wants to keep busy so she went in today. She said everybody's been sweet, offering to help. John, well…" She shrugged. "I'm still waiting for it to really hit him."

"How 'bout the kids?"

"Kyle's heartbroken, but he's trying to be brave. When I try to talk to Emily about it, she just goes back to her dolls."

Her chin wavered, and Matt put a hand on her shoulder. He suspected that, in her own way, Emily was trying to be brave like her brother. As they all were.

"You're doing a great job. Just hang in there."

She gave him a watery smile. "Thanks."

They sipped their coffee, and suddenly Matt realized

things hadn't gone as far downhill as they usually did when the two of them were together for more than two minutes.

"Are we actually having a pleasant conversation?" he asked.

"What do you mean?" she demanded. "We have lots of pleasant conversations."

"They start out that way, then we end up yelling at each other."

"We do not."

"And it's a race to see who can get outta the room first," he finished evenly.

"That's not true." After another sip of coffee, though, she giggled the way she used to when she was a little girl. "Yes, it is. I guess we're a lot alike."

"You make that sound like it's a bad thing," he teased.

"Sometimes it is."

When her smile faded, he braced himself for part two of the scolding he'd gotten before their morning prayer. Even though she was frowning at him, he was surprised to see honest sympathy in her eyes. "I wish you could just try—"

"Well, I can't," he said as gently as he could. "I don't expect you to understand."

"Life is so much harder without faith, Matt."

"You've got plenty of faith," he reminded her. "Did it make your husband taking off any easier for you?"

"Yes, it did. I trusted God to take care of us, and He did."

"*You* took care of you, and the kids. God had nothing to do with it."

Smiling, Marianne shook her head. "He had everything to do with it. He gave me the strength I needed to leave Chicago and come back here. He blessed me with a family that would take me in and love my children. Without Him, we'd have been completely lost."

Meaning she thought he was lost, Matt realized. Out of respect for their new truce, he opted not to debate religion with her. He was grateful when John came through the back door and flopped into a chair, making a small cloud of dust. Without being asked, Marianne got up and filled a glass with ice and water.

"Thanks," he croaked. Within ten seconds the glass was empty and refilled.

"Man, that tastes good."

"I wish you would have taken today off," she chided him, running a motherly hand through his sweaty hair. "You look exhausted."

"No help for it. We've got just as much work and four fewer pairs of hands."

John was by nature a helpless optimist. Hearing him sound so discouraged made Matt wonder how he'd ever get through the rest of the harvest. Hoping to lighten the mood, Matt asked, "You leave anything for me to do?"

"A few tons of hay, most of the corn. The hay can wait, but from the looks of it we've only got a few days on the corn."

"That old harvester up and running?"

Grimacing, John shook his head. "Engine keeps quitting on us. Dad—"

He stopped abruptly, glancing at Marianne. She patted his arm with a smile. "It's okay, John. Go ahead."

"Dad thought it might be electrical, but he wasn't sure."

"I'll have a look, see what it needs."

"How're things at Caty's?" John asked as he fished three cookies out of the jar in the middle of the table.

"The place is a mess," Matt answered. "But she's fixed on staying there. There's no electricity, so I invited her out later for a shower and something to eat."

John and Marianne traded an odd look, and Matt asked, "What?"

"Nothing," John replied, clearly trying to keep back a smile but failing miserably. "That was nice of you."

"She's helping us with Dad's estate. I figured it was the least I could do."

John's infernal grin widened, but before Matt could say anything, John polished off his water and stood up. "I'd best get back to it."

After the screen door slapped shut behind him, Matt turned to his sister. "Why do y'all smile when I mention Caty?"

"We all like her," she said.

When she artfully changed the subject to which of Ruthy's concoctions she should thaw for dessert that night, Matt decided Marianne wasn't going to answer him.

The cranky old harvester wouldn't cooperate for more than thirty seconds at a time. With oil-stained fingers, Matt paged through the dog-eared maintenance manual, searching for answers. He even tried kicking the machine a few times, which only made it sputter to a stop. After spending the afternoon baling the back hayfield with John, this was the last thing he needed. Muttering to himself, he decided to call it a day. Maybe if he quit thinking about it, the solution would come to him.

On his way to the house, he noticed John sitting on the top step of his small porch. Arms draped over his legs, he was staring at the ground. He looked completely defeated and, tired as Matt was, he couldn't just leave him there.

Changing direction, Matt walked down the well-beaten path to the carriage house, using the time to come up with something brilliant to say.

"Hey, there," was the best he could do.

When John lifted his head, his dusty face was streaked with tears. Matt sat down beside his little brother, wishing he knew what to say.

"I should've seen it," John groaned in a ragged voice. "It was too hot. I should've made him stop."

"It wasn't your fault. Even if you'd said something, he wouldn't have quit. You know that."

"Just a few more passes," he lamented. "We'd have been done."

"I know."

After that, there wasn't much left to say. So he listened, letting John pour out the sorrow that must have been choking him for days now.

When his tears subsided, he lifted his head and gave Matt a weak smile. "Sorry."

"Don't worry about it. Come on up and have something to eat."

"In a while."

John's gaze wandered a bit, settling on the ancient oak tree their father had loved so much. Matt had a pretty good idea what he was thinking, but no profound words came to mind. Patting his brother's shoulder, Matt left him alone with his memories.

After a quick shower, Matt settled at the kitchen table with the newspaper. Out in the yard, Tucker started barking like a maniac, and Matt glanced out to find Caty's MG pulling in beside his truck. She stepped out and greeted the Lab with a thorough ruffling of both ears. When he reared up and plunked his paws on her hips, she laughed and hugged him back.

The dog retreated and spun in circles while Caty fished a backpack from the passenger seat and settled it on her shoulder. Obviously thrilled with their company, Tucker trotted alongside her, tongue wagging as if he'd been waiting a month for her to come back. Apparently, the entire family had a weakness for Caty McKenzie.

Including Matt, it seemed.

Driving the tractor up and down countless rows of hay, he had kept wondering how her rehab work was going. Crazy as her plan was, he couldn't help admiring her willingness to leave the past behind and move on. He didn't know her that well, but any fool could see she hadn't been happy in Charlotte. Once the shock wore off, he'd wager she'd actually be glad she'd lost her job. He'd had more than a few jobs like that, so he understood.

Gazing out across the seemingly endless fields waiting to be harvested, he had tensed up reflexively. Willing his muscles to relax, he had reminded himself he wasn't staying. John and the girls just needed him to bridge the gap until they adjusted. Three months, and he was gone.

"Knock, knock!"

Caty's face appeared in the screen, and he got up to open the door. "You missed a spot," he teased, rubbing a smudge of dirt off her cheek.

"There's plenty more where that came from," she warned, staying on the porch. "You might want to hose me off before you let me in."

Marianne laughed. "Don't be silly. You're cleaner than the hounds and field hands that traipse through here every day."

"Upstairs bathroom or down?" Caty asked.

"Down. Kyle left an experiment going in the upstairs tub. Something to do with submarines and diving bells," Marianne added, rolling her eyes.

"Sounds interesting. I'll have to go check it out."

The bathroom door closed behind her, and Marianne turned to Matt with a curious look. "You like her, don't you?"

"Sure," he said noncommittally, tossing a scrap of corn-bread to the furry beggar beside the counter. "Not as much as Tucker does, though."

"John thinks she hangs the moon, you know."

"Yeah, I noticed." He left out the part about it bothering him. He still didn't understand why, and he didn't want his nosy sister reading anything into it. "Are they together?"

"No," Marianne said with obvious regret. "Even back in high school, she kept telling him she wanted to stay friends. I think he finally gave up sometime last year."

She took a casserole dish out of the oven and set it in a handled frame on the counter. The she turned to smirk at him. "You really didn't remember her?"

Great. She and Caty must have had a good laugh over that one. "Eventually I did. In my defense, I was in high school when she moved here."

"Not an excuse when a lady's involved," John said as he came through the back door and planted a kiss on Mari-anne's cheek. "Something smells great."

"Mystery casserole." With a fond smile, she reached up to ruffle his damp hair. "You look much better than you did at lunch."

"I feel better. Thanks again, Matt."

"Anytime."

Caty came out of the bathroom and hung her backpack over the basement doorknob. Her hair looped up in a damp ponytail, she was dressed in frayed denim shorts and a faded Boston College T-shirt. Somehow, she looked just as good that way as she had in her high-powered lawyer clothes.

Without asking, she opened the cupboard and started taking out dishes. "How many?"

"The kids are down at the Millers', and Lisa should be here soon, so five. How are things at your place?"

"Cleaner, but there's still a lot to do. My electric just came on, and Frank Hastings took care of the mice."

Marianne did a girly shiver. "I hate those things. Scrambling around, chasing each other all over the place. They give me the willies."

"They don't eat much," Caty said as she started laying out the plates. "Marianne, do you have any twin-size sheets and a pillow I could borrow? Gram wrapped my old mattress in plastic so it's fine, but all the linens are full of holes."

Leaning over his sister's shoulder, John mimicked the sound of gnawing rodents. She smacked him with a wooden spoon, which only made him laugh.

"Over there," she ordered, pointing at the table with her spoon.

"Yes'm." Grinning like an idiot, he flung himself into the chair next to Matt's. When he saw Matt was reading the sports section, he shoved in for a look. "How'd the Braves do?"

"Lost their shirts. They need a couple guys who can hit home runs every once in a while."

"And a catcher who doesn't use a walker. They better come up with something fast or they'll miss the play-offs."

While they lamented the team's many shortcomings, Marianne and Caty continued their conversation at the counter.

"If you don't mind Transformers, you can borrow some of Kyle's sheets," Marianne said.

"Thanks a bunch. Clean Transformers are way better than what I've got."

Lisa opened the door and joined them with a puzzled expression. "What's this about Transformers?"

They explained, and she said, "Honey, can I ask you

something?" When Caty nodded, she went on. "You usually stay at the B and B when you visit. What's going on?"

Caty looked over at Matt, but he kept his expression neutral. It was her story to tell, but only if she wanted to. He'd made a promise, and he had no intention of breaking it.

She curled up in a chair like a cat, wrapping her arms around her legs. "There's something y'all should know." Leaving out the gory details, she filled them in on what had brought her back to Harland. "Right now I'm concentrating on the house. I've got some money saved, so I should be okay until I can get an office put together and start seeing clients."

"How do you manage that?" Matt heard himself ask. When the others looked confused, he added, "Stay so positive, I mean. You've got a ton of hard work ahead of you, but it sounds to me like you're looking forward to it."

"You keep your eye on the prize," she answered immediately. "All the steps along the way are worth the effort if you're going toward something you really want."

Her eyes were locked with his, the encouragement in her voice like a warm touch on his skin. Unsettled by the feeling, he fought back with logic. "What if you can't have what you really want?"

Completely unfazed, she met his pessimism with a smile. "Then you make the best of things."

After chewing on that for a few seconds, he chuckled. "Can't argue with that."

"Good," she approved with a laugh. "Pass the sweet tea, please."

Chapter Five

The next morning, Caty woke up to muted sunlight coming into her childhood bedroom. She'd left the window open all night, enjoying the fresh air and chirping crickets. She never could have done that in Charlotte, partly because the burglar alarm would have kept going off and partly because the nonstop traffic would have kept her awake.

But in Harland, even here in the middle of town, she'd gotten the best night's sleep she'd had in months. Stretching lazily, she watched the emerging sun for a while, admiring the way the sky changed from streaky pink to warm oranges and yellows. If she tipped her head just right, the bank of puffy clouds outside her window looked like a French poodle with a bow on its tail.

Caty smiled at her own foolishness. When was the last time she'd just lain in bed like this? While she often watched the sunrise, she was always sitting on her back steps with a cup of coffee, scrolling through new emails and messages. An occasional occurrence that had morphed into a habit, it gave her a jump on things but didn't allow her to ease into the day the way she preferred.

Now that the electric was back on, she had water. Sort of. The kitchen faucet was the newest, so she'd started there. After fifteen minutes, the murky sludge had given way to something resembling rusty Kool-Aid. Not ideal, but it would get better. It beat having no water at all. She hated to think what might come out of the much older bathroom fixtures. Picking up her phone, she opened her list and typed in "replace showerhead" and "buy pillow and sheets."

Pressing Play on her iPod dock, she plumped up her pillow and leaned back against the old wrought-iron headboard. As one country song blended into the next, she let her mind drift. Unfortunately, her mind wasn't used to having so much uncommitted time, and twenty minutes of leisure was more than enough.

She got out of bed and pulled some clean clothes from her suitcase. The reflection in the grimy mirror was nothing to brag about, but there wasn't much she could do beyond knotting her hair into a ponytail. She stripped the bed and folded Kyle's sheets back into the pillowcase. Tucking her phone in the pocket of her shorts, she carried the sheets downstairs so she wouldn't forget to return them.

The stairs creaked in a few new places, but it was a comfortable, familiar sound. Although she'd been in Charlotte almost a year, she'd never warmed up to the ultramodern steel-and-glass buildings so common in its busy downtown. She much preferred old buildings with a sense of history. When she walked into the kitchen, there were several gallon jugs of water on the counter. Marianne had insisted she take them with her last night, along with a bar of soap, a scrubber sponge and a roll of paper towels. Now Caty was glad to have them.

She scrubbed the sink as well as she could and filled it to wash her face. The cool water freshened her skin, and she poured some into her travel mug to drink. Then she realized she'd made a very serious mistake.

No coffee.

Groaning out loud, she closed her eyes and wished for a mocha caramel latte to start what promised to be another long day. It didn't work. When she opened them, she was still holding a cup of water.

Mentally kicking herself, she unlocked the front door. At first tug, it wouldn't budge. Setting her cup down, she grasped the old brass knob with both hands and gave it a good yank. That broke the swollen door free, and it swung open with a jarring screech from the hinges.

"WD-40." Echoing Matt's advice, she picked up her water and strolled out onto the front porch. *Her* front porch, she thought with a grin. Not a tiny stoop like the one she had in Charlotte, with barely enough space for a potted plant. No, this one was deep and ran the whole front of the house. It called out for a swing and some comfy chairs that would encourage people to come up and visit awhile.

Pinpoints of light shone on the old floorboards, and she looked up to find what must have been dozens of holes in the roof. They were circled by rust stains, which told her the old tin had been pulling away from the nails holding it in place. She could sand, paint and stain with the best of them, manage some minor repairs if she had to. But she didn't know the first thing about roofs, so she'd have to hire someone who did. Sighing, she added it to her rapidly growing list.

On the bright side, the porch would look great once she'd painted the old boards and bought some crisp white wicker furniture. Imagining where she'd put things, she spun in a slow circle. That was when she noticed something on the steps. It was a red toolbox with a pink bow and a Harland Hardware business card tied to the handle. Inside were all the basics: hammer, pliers, several different screwdrivers, nuts, bolts, nails. Under the pullout tray she found a small pair of leather work gloves and a copy of the phone book for Harland and several surrounding towns.

"What a great idea," she murmured, wondering who'd thought of it. Lifting the book out, she found a compact first-aid kit.

There was no signature anywhere, but the last item was a dead giveaway. Matt was the only person in Harland who'd be up early enough—and had the wry humor—to leave her a present like this. Jewelry was nice, and she really liked getting flowers, but he was the only guy she knew who'd give her anything even remotely practical.

She scrolled to his number on her phone and was surprised when he answered on the first ring.

"Mornin'," he greeted her over a purring engine in the background.

"Good morning to you, too. I thought you'd be out in the cornfield."

"Later I will. I've been fighting with this old harvester since five."

"What's wrong with it?"

"Everything," he growled.

"It sounds good now," she complimented him. "I wanted to thank you for the toolbox. The bandages and liquid sutures were a nice touch."

He laughed. "Thought you'd appreciate that. You get into anything dangerous, put it down and call somebody, okay?"

"Like who?"

"Me or John, plumber, electrician, ambulance, whatever. Just be careful," he added in a suddenly somber tone. "Some things are better left to the pros."

He had a point there, she thought as she glanced up at the porch roof. She wasn't helpless, but she wasn't exactly Miss Fix-it, either. "Don't worry. I know my limits."

"Glad to hear it." The engine shut off, and he came back on the line. "I hate to cut this short, but some o' this corn's ready to drop off the stalks, and it looks like rain."

"Good luck."

"Thanks." He gave a short laugh and hung up.

After a quick inventory, Caty updated her list and headed out. The sky darkened by the minute and by the time she got back home, it was pouring. In her driveway, water streaming between the broken sections of concrete was forming a swamp in the front yard. At least it still drained away from the house, she mused with a sigh.

The rain would quit soon, she reasoned, so she forwarded her iPod to her favorite new song and sat back to wait it out. She just happened to glance through the driver's window at the house. Then she looked again.

Her front porch was stacked with boxes.

The leaky roof wasn't much protection from the rain, and water pelted the cartons, loaded with her precious books. She'd collected legal reference volumes throughout law school and afterward, and many were out of print now. Then there were the original editions she'd inherited, from Cooper's *Leatherstocking Tales* to one of the first published copies of Galileo's discoveries. Leather bound and rarer than rare, they were irreplaceable.

She had to get them inside, but she'd never be able to move those boxes. The hardware store would have thick tarps, though. Just as she was restarting her car, her phone rang and she glanced at the caller ID. Matt. It wasn't the perfect solution, but it was better than nothing.

Glancing up, she smiled her thanks and hit the answer button. "Hey, there."

"We're calling it a day, so I thought I'd see how things are going at your haunted house."

"You have excellent timing."

"I've heard that before," he said with a chuckle.

She decided to ignore that. "I could really use your help." Caty explained her predicament, ending with, "I hate to bug you, but it's pouring and I have a lot of books."

"On my way."

The line went dead, and she imagined him jumping into his big blue truck, racing into town to come to her rescue.

"Oh, Caty," she chided herself as she braced for a drenching, "you really have to cut back on those romance novels."

She slogged through the marshy front yard and ran up the porch steps. In a plastic sleeve on one of the boxes she found a soggy invoice from the moving company. Tucked in with it was a note scrawled on the back of a Dunkin' Donuts napkin.

Nobody home. Left shipment as requested.

To be fair, she had told the movers they could put some of the boxes on the front porch, since she'd need time to make space for everything in the small house. She'd paid extra for heavy-duty cartons for her books, with explicit instructions to bring them inside. What moron left such heavy boxes with a female customer who couldn't possibly manage them on her own?

To make matters worse, she'd made the arrangements with the moving company before she knew the roof leaked, and her stuff wasn't supposed to arrive until Monday. Later she'd call and give them the lawyer treatment, but that wouldn't solve the immediate problem of rescuing her books from the rain.

When she tried to unlock the front door, the old mechanism resisted. Frustrated, she torqued on it and got it to turn. Just as the lock freed up, there was a grating squeal as the old key snapped in two. Perfect.

Sighing, she hefted several smaller boxes, hunting

for something she could drag into the living room. She couldn't care less about her clothes. They could be washed or dry-cleaned and be no worse for the rain. But with each pelting raindrop, she imagined dry pages wicking up water and curling in their bindings.

One carton actually moved when she tugged on it, scraping across the neglected floorboards. It got hung up on the threshold, and she crouched down to boost it over. When she finally shoved it into place beside the door, she stopped to catch her breath. It was a good thing Matt was coming to help her. She'd have a snowball's chance in Maui of managing this job on her own.

Just as she was pushing another box inside, Matt pulled into her driveway. Instructing her to take the ones labeled "clothes," he asked, "Where to?"

"The kitchen. They can stay in there while I work on the living room."

"Yes, ma'am."

His day had started long before hers, and he must have been exhausted. Still, he lugged in box after box of books without complaint. She knew they were heavy—she'd barely been able to scoot a smallish one across the floor. But he made them look as though they weighed nothing at all. No doubt about it, he was a handy guy to have around.

As he went over to the sink to wash his hands, she stood in the archway, eyes fixed on the biggest surprise she'd gotten from him so far. High on his right shoulder, framed by his gray workout tank, was a tattoo of an eagle. Wings outstretched, the drawing was so detailed it looked as if it could actually take flight. The fact that it was wrapped around a very impressive biceps only added to the effect.

When he turned around, he frowned. "What?"

"Nothing." Busted. She felt her cheeks warming, and

she figured it was best to come clean. "That's a neat tattoo."

"Neat, huh?" He chuckled as he unwound some paper towels and dried his hands. "I'll tell Moose. He's always dying for a compliment."

"How long have you had it?" she couldn't help asking.

Grinning, he tossed the towel in the trash. "You mean, has my family seen it? Only John so far. I've had it awhile, though. Doesn't show unless I want it to."

"You wanted me to see it?"

"I didn't mind if you did." He braced his hands on either side of the sink and leaned back. "Does it bother you?"

Caty wasn't usually into things like that, body art and piercings and such. Most people overdid them, canceling out the *cool* factor. Matt's suited him, but she wasn't ready to tell him that. "That depends. Are there any more?"

His grin turned wicked, his eyes twinkling with uncharacteristic mischief. Who'd have guessed dark, intense Matt Sawyer had a playful side?

"Forget I asked," she retorted, laughing in spite of herself. "But I hope you'll let me buy you lunch."

"Not a chance. I'd never let a lady pay."

There was that chivalrous streak again. She couldn't decide if it was charming or insulting.

Frowning, he looked around her kitchen, made even smaller by the stacks of boxes. "You want some help making a path in here so you can use this kitchen?"

Caty shrugged. For her, a working kitchen was pretty far down the list. "I'm not much of a cook. Gram tried, but I'm a total klutz in the kitchen."

"Ruthy's, then?"

Just hearing the woman's name made her stomach growl. "Definitely."

When they walked back into the living room, she

frowned. She didn't think she had that much stuff, but the space seemed to have shrunk in the last hour. Caty pushed aside the negative thought and turned to Matt with a smile. "Thanks so much for your help. Those books would've gotten ruined on my leaky front porch."

"No problem." Looking around at the disheveled state of her house, he chuckled. "This must make your Charlotte place look pretty good."

Actually, it was the reverse. Her beautiful town house could have belonged to anyone, and it had never really suited her. That was a little more personal information than she wanted to share with him, so she shrugged.

"You didn't like Charlotte?" he pressed.

"I'm not sure."

"How long were you there?"

She felt her cheeks warming again. "Almost a year."

"You're kidding. And no boyfriend?"

"I've been really, really busy."

Matt stared at her as if she had an extra head. "I never met a woman who couldn't make time for a boyfriend."

"Now you have." She forced a smile to make it seem like no big deal.

"Who was he?"

"Who?"

"The guy," he continued, folding his arms and looking very dangerous. "The last one you made time for."

There was no point in hedging. It wasn't a big deal, and she wasn't ashamed of it or anything. "He's in Boston, happily married and waiting to be a father."

"What happened?"

"Nothing. We just weren't right for each other." Matt cocked his head, disbelief written all over his face. "Don't give me that look. That's all you're getting."

He gave her a devilish grin. "I've heard that before."

"I'm sure you have. How 'bout I just tell you you're bad and you can quit trying to shock me."

"Deal."

Laughing, she shook a scolding finger at him. "You're a bad, bad man, Matthew."

But he wasn't laughing. He caught her hand against his chest, pulling her closer. His eyes blazed a deep, brilliant blue she'd never seen in her life, and the sudden intensity actually knocked the breath out of her. Under her hand, his heart beat out a rhythm that pounded through her entire body.

She had no doubt he could snap her arm like a twig, but he cradled her hand as though it was something fragile. She should have been terrified, but she wasn't, which made no sense at all.

Thrown completely off balance, she struggled to talk normally. "What?"

"No one ever calls me that," he murmured. "Why would you?"

"It's your name," she stammered, fumbling for composure.

"No one ever calls me that," he repeated. A smile slowly spread across his tanned features, settling in to twinkle in those remarkable eyes. "I like the way you say it."

Her brain was totally locked, focused on the warmth in his gaze, the strong hand covering hers. Abruptly, something changed, and she watched storm clouds blow through his eyes. They shifted to a troubled gray, and he took a step away from her. A large step.

"You must be starving. Let's eat."

Matt strode past her and out the front door before Caty could put any coherent words together. She looked at her bewildered reflection in the grimy entryway mirror and shook her head. Whatever had just happened, she had to put it out of her mind. She and Matt would be working together on his father's estate, she reminded herself as she closed the front door behind her. She had to keep things professional, for both their sakes.

"You didn't lock the front door," he scolded before she was even settled.

Still distracted by whatever had just happened, she registered his disapproval but not the words. Turning to face him, she asked, "What?"

"You didn't lock the front door," he repeated more gently. "Something wrong with it?"

"Kind of," she said lightly. "There's a broken key stuck in it."

"You should get it replaced. I know this is Harland, but a woman living alone should have locks on her doors."

"I know that. I'm not a moron."

She cringed when she heard the sharp edge on her voice. He'd gone out of his way to help her, and here she was biting his head off for being concerned about her safety. "I'm sorry, Matt. I didn't mean to snarl at you."

"No problem," Matt replied as they headed for Main Street. "You okay?"

"Peachy."

"Everything's gonna be all right, y'know. We'll figure something out."

The way he phrased it grated on her, and she snapped, "None of this is your problem. I can take care of myself."

He glowered at her, blue and gray swirling impatiently in his eyes. "So I'm only good for hauling heavy boxes?"

"Forgive me for ruining your day," she shot back. "I've never done this before, so I'm not up on the protocol."

Muttering things she'd rather not have heard, he heaved such a big sigh the eagle on his shoulder looked ready to take off.

When he glanced over again, he was wearing a wry grin. "We're a lot alike, you and me. Y'know that?"

She wasn't falling for the deadly Sawyer charm. She folded her arms and scowled at him, even though his eyes were on the road and he couldn't see her expression. "How do you mean?"

"We hate asking for help. When we have to, it makes us mean, 'cause we feel like a failure."

When he said it, she knew that last word summed up everything she was feeling. She'd failed to do her job well, failed to recognize something was wrong. Failed to plan for the possibility that she might fail.

That was a lot of failure.

"Don't worry," he said as he pulled in at the diner. "You'll get used to it."

"Failing?"

"Getting past it." Shutting off the engine, he turned to face her. "Just takes a little practice, is all. I'm guessing you haven't had much."

"I try to avoid it."

"Well, I've had plenty and it didn't kill me. Won't kill you, either."

He gave her an encouraging smile. She tried to return the gesture, but her heart wasn't quite in it. "Thanks."

"Anytime."

He came around to open her door for her, then reached behind the seat and grabbed a faded blue T-shirt. After tugging it on, he stepped back and they hurried through the rain to cross the street.

A blue-and-white-striped awning covered the front of Ruthy's Place and, despite the rain, underneath it was dry. The door was open, and wonderful smells wafted out toward the sidewalk. Caty had often suspected that a fan system blew the scent of comfort food outside to lure customers into the diner.

Now that they were out of the rain, she paused to ask, "Why are you so intent on hiding that tattoo? You know someone's going to see it eventually."

"Maybe, maybe not."

He gave her a cocky grin, and she shook her head. "You're hopeless."

The grin widened, making it clear he took that as a compliment. "More or less."

"What am I going to do with you? Wait," she interrupted as he opened his mouth. "Don't answer that."

For the first time since his father's funeral, he laughed. Not the reserved, contained sound she'd heard before, but an actual, heartfelt laugh. Knowing she was the one who'd managed to coax it from him made her smile.

Matt motioned her ahead of him, and she stepped into a homey place that welcomed customers with the restaurant version of a hug. If a building could have a personality, this one would be eternally cheerful. The decor was classic country, with pale blue walls and ruffled yellow gingham curtains framing the windows. A high shelf ran the entire perimeter of the walls, providing a home for the owner's eclectic collection of antique kitchenware and knickknacks. In the place of honor over the door was a ceramic figure of Ruthy's beloved terrier Lucy. Life-size.

Two waitresses zoomed in on Matt and raced to get to him first.

"I don't think so," Lisa announced from behind the counter, shooing them away.

Lisa led Caty and Matt to an isolated table in the corner. Wearing a pink dress and ruffled white apron, she looked like herself again. On closer inspection, Caty noticed her friend's makeup was a little heavier than usual. That was

Lisa, she mused fondly. Soldiering on, armed with mascara and lip gloss.

"Thanks, Lise," Matt said with a wry grin.

"No problem," she answered, handing them each a menu. "What can I get you to drink?"

Matt ordered a pitcher of sweet tea and opened the menu as though nothing out of the ordinary had just happened.

"Do women often kill each other to get to you?" Caty asked as she ignored the menu and studied the specials board. That was where Ruthy listed her latest inventions, and they were always worth trying.

"Not really."

She laughed. "Why don't I believe that?"

"'Cause you're the suspicious type. Goes with the lawyer package."

She *hmm*ed at that and ordered a Country Club sandwich to go with his loaded bacon cheeseburger. He filled her glass and lounged back with his own. "So, once you're done rescuing that wreck of a house, what are your plans?"

"I always meant to come back here and open my own firm. Maybe God saw me on the wrong path and steered me back, so I could do what He meant for me to do all along."

As soon as it was out of her mouth, she knew it was the wrong thing to say to Matt. To his credit, he didn't shoot her down. He just sat there and listened while she thought out loud.

"Grandpa's workroom is on the side of the house, connected but with a separate entrance. Once I fix it up, it will be a great office. My rates would have to be pretty low, but I own the house, so if I'm careful I shouldn't have too many expenses." She paused for a bite of her sandwich. "What do you think?"

Without hesitation, he smiled. "I think anyone who

could get through more than one Boston winter could do anything they set their mind to."

"I've had a few offers on the house over the years, but I wanted to keep a connection to Harland, so I held on to it. It just needs some TLC."

That made him laugh like a maniac, and she scowled at him. "What's so funny?"

"I guess your version of TLC and mine are a little different."

"Obviously," she said, as Lisa came to see how they were doing.

"Caty, is he hassling you?" she asked.

"Incessantly."

"Yeah, he's got a knack for that." With a mock scowl, she balled up the check and tossed it at him. Then she turned on her heel and strolled away.

Matt popped a fry in his mouth, and washed it down with some tea. "You're really set on doing this, aren't you?"

"Yes, I am," she told him in the same determined tone she'd used when she'd informed Grandpa that, yes, she was going to law school up north with a bunch of Yankees. In the snow.

"Well, good luck, sweetheart."

"I'll be fine. And quit calling me sweetheart," she added with a huff. "Think of something else."

A slow grin spread across his face, and he nodded. "Okay."

She couldn't imagine what he found so amusing, and honestly she didn't care. She was finally home to stay. That was all that mattered.

"Sure," Caty grumbled later that afternoon. "Now it quits raining."

She was in the kitchen unloading her books. A few of

the covers were damp, and she fanned the pages to make sure they didn't need drying. She'd been stacking them on the counters but quickly ran out of space. She hated to put them on the floor, and she certainly couldn't leave them in the wet boxes. Then she had a brainstorm.

The laundry room. A hallway ran the width of the house, separating the living room and kitchen from Grandpa's workroom and the laundry room. It wasn't large, but it had a long counter and lots of shelves where Gram had stored her canning jars. Armload by armload, Caty carted books through the house, lining them up on the shelves so she could see the titles. With the house a long way from being organized, they might be in here awhile, and she wanted to be able to find a book if she needed it.

When she was done, she closed the door to keep out the dust she'd inevitably be creating with her various projects.

"One job down, a million to go," she said out loud, swallowing some water from the bottle she'd left on the newel post.

While she was debating what to do next, she heard a clanking out on the porch. She opened the front door to find Matt there with a toolbox and a sledgehammer. He looked like he meant business.

"Whatcha doin'?" she asked casually, leaning against the door frame.

"Brought you this." Leaning down, he pulled a brand-new set of locks from a hardware bag. "I got 'em for the other two doors, too. I'm figuring you've never installed a dead-bolt lock."

"You figured right." She reached for the package, but he pulled it away. "I can read, Matt. I'm sure I can manage."

"How are you with a drill and a spade bit?"

"A what?"

He grinned, and she had to laugh. She must have

sounded like a complete idiot. "Fine, you can replace my locks. What's all that?" she asked when she noticed sheets of white aluminum in the back of his truck.

"Your new roof," he replied, as if it was obvious.

She had to admit, they'd look a lot nicer than the rusty old ones she had now. "Where did you get those?"

"Found 'em in one of our barns. Ground's still soaked, so I thought I'd do some inventory, see what we've got. There's not enough of these to be any use at the farm, but I think they'll work here."

Caty didn't know what to make of his generous offer. He could have taken advantage of the rare time off to relax or watch TV or something, but he'd come to help her instead. "I really appreciate you doing this. If you need anything, let me know."

"I'm good."

The whirring of the drill moved around the house as he went from door to door. Before long it stopped altogether. When she heard the clang of his truck's tailgate, she knew he was bringing in the long panels. Even though he'd made it clear he could handle the job on his own, she didn't feel right packing china in Bubble Wrap when he was out there doing real work.

Through the screen she asked, "Can I help? Hold the ladder or something?"

"Demo's fun," he said with a grin. "You'll need gloves, though."

"I just happen to have some." Grabbing them from the toolbox on the kitchen counter, she met him out front.

On the porch, he set the ladder in place and stepped back so she could climb up high enough to reach the roof. When she was balanced, he offered her the sledgehammer. It weighed a lot more than she'd expected, but she got control of it and took a few tentative whacks at the underside of the roof. Most of the nails had rusted clear through, and after a few more swings the center panel slid to the ground with a satisfying screech. Before she knew it, Caty was drenched in sweat and her porch was roofless.

"Nice job," Matt approved, high-fiving her.

"That was fun!" Jumping down, she handed him the sledge. "What else have you got?"

"Once I get a panel or two nailed in, you can come up and help with the rest. You know how to use a hammer?"

Tilting her head back, she looked him square in the eyes and gave him the wilting look she practiced in the mirror when she had to go to court.

He chuckled. "How 'bout this? I handle the aluminum, you do the nailing."

"Sounds good. In the meantime, I'll hand the panels up to you."

From his stern expression, she thought he might tell her to stand back and stay out of his way. But the blue in his eyes warmed a little, and he gave her a crooked grin. "Thanks."

"You're welcome."

The pieces weren't all that heavy, and she slid the first one up to him, then another. It didn't take him long to make a platform, and she handed the rest of the panels up before joining him on the roof. Standing, she looked out over the town with a smile. She could see the war monument in the square, bordered by the churches. Gus was headed somewhere, his Model T delivery truck piled high with lumber. The playground was full of kids making the most of the last weekend of their summer vacation.

Harland, with its simple charm and easy pace, was truly where she belonged. She couldn't believe it had taken her so long to figure that out. "It's even prettier from up here."

Matt responded with some particularly loud banging.

When he finished, Caty crouched down beside him. "You really hate it here, don't you?"

"Mmm-hmm," he said around the nails sticking out of his mouth.

"Do you think you'll ever change your mind?"

He didn't say anything, but his dark expression answered her as clearly as any words.

Chapter Six

The rest of the week was a blur of very early starts and finishing in the hazy glow of tractor headlights, but they got the corn in while the weather held. Matt hadn't had time to hire anyone to replace the guys they'd lost, so they were seriously shorthanded. It was like running a marathon, harvesting, sorting, and filling truck after brimming truck to be taken to the feed distributor ten miles away.

Finally, he ran the last load out and parked the empty truck in the barn. He should have cleaned out the back, but he was just too tired. Dragging himself into the house, he showered and pulled on some clean clothes. Then, for lack of anything better to do, he wandered aimlessly through the house.

The kids' rooms were neat as a pin, beds made and every toy in its place. The cool evening breeze rustled through the curtains on the windows, white lace in Emily's room, green plaid in Kyle's. Marianne's door was closed, and he heard his sisters' muffled voices inside. On the other side of the bathroom, at the end of the hall, the front bedroom door stood half-open, the way it had for as long as he could remember.

Matt stared at it for what felt like a long time. Drawn by

something he couldn't explain, he strolled down the hall and through the door.

The room was just the way his father had left it, somewhere between tidy and cluttered. The bed was unmade, his bathrobe tossed across the foot of it. Work clothes were draped over the back of an old wooden chair, and a devotional book lay open on the bedside table. Curious about what his father had been reading the day he died, Matt picked up the book.

The heading of the page summed up his father's philosophy of life. "If you can believe, all things are possible." Underneath were stories about people who had beaten the odds and achieved things even they had thought were impossible. A paralyzed teenager walked to the podium to get his high school diploma. After ten years of trying, an infertile couple conceived twins. A woman searched for twelve years and finally found the father who hadn't even known she existed.

That one made him think of Caty. He wondered why she hadn't made an effort to find her own father. Then again, it really wasn't any of his business. As he set the book down, he noticed beside it, where it had always been, Dad's favorite picture in its tarnished silver frame.

It was the last family photo taken before Mom had gotten sick. The six of them sat on a checked blanket beside the church, enjoying a picnic. Lisa was a toddler on their mother's lap, laughing at whoever was holding the camera. John was sprawled out as usual, opposite Matt, who looked over his shoulder at the photographer. A pigtailed Marianne hung over Dad's shoulder, a huge grin on her face.

Even though it was more than twenty years ago, he remembered that day so clearly he could smell the fried chicken. Staring down at his mother's face, he saw himself in her dark hair and deep blue eyes. The others were pure

Sawyer, with light brown hair and pale blue eyes. More than once Matt had caught his dad looking at him with a sad expression. When Matt got older, he understood that he reminded his father of the woman he'd loved and lost much too young.

Giving your heart to someone left you open to that kind of pain, Matt thought as he set the picture back in its place. That was why he always kept his distance.

These were the memories that had driven him away fifteen years ago. He'd been keeping busy, trying to stay ahead of them. But they'd snuck up on him and caught him from behind.

If he didn't get out of here, he knew they'd drag him down and never let him back up.

Without a word to anyone, Matt climbed into his truck and started driving. It didn't matter where he went, so long as it was away from the farm and the crushing memories that had been waiting in the shadows to ambush him.

He'd last come home two Christmases ago. He'd stayed too long at a friend's party and been late for Marianne's traditional Christmas Eve feast. By the time he'd gotten there, the eggnog was gone and Ethan was wearing the red-and-green reindeer pajamas the kids had made him open early.

"Merry Christmas, Matt," he'd said as the clock chimed midnight. "Are you hungry?"

A lifelong farmer, Dad was always early to bed, early to rise, but that night he'd stayed up to see Matt. John and Lisa had gone home, and Marianne and the kids were in bed. Matt and his father rummaged through the leftovers, filling their plates with everything from pulled pork to Christmas cookies. Washing it down with root beer, they had one of those everything-and-nothing conservations you never really appreciate until you realize it was the last one.

What did they talk about? Matt wondered, reaching for details but coming up empty. It was their last face-to-face, and he couldn't recall anything. Close on the heels of that thought was one that made him feel even worse.

If he'd been in touch with his family, he'd have known they were bringing the hay in. He could have come down to lend a hand, as he used to do.

If he'd been there, their father would still be alive.

The violent force behind that thought caught him off guard, and he realized he had the steering wheel in a death grip. He also realized he had no clue how he'd gotten where he was, and he had no business driving right now. Fortunately he was near Caty's house, and he pulled into her washed-out driveway before he wrecked his truck. Or worse.

Delayed panic set in, and his heart started banging against his ribs as if it meant to slam right through his chest. Leaning his head back against the headrest, he took in a deep breath and held it before letting it out. After repeating that a few times, he felt calmer but not exactly normal. Then again, maybe *normal* was a relative term.

A motion to his left caught his eye, and he swiveled his head to find Caty's worried face outside. Lowering the window, he did his best to smile. "Hey, there."

"Hey, yourself. Are you okay?"

"Define *okay*."

Her half smile told him that even though he hadn't said much, she completely understood what he meant. When she opened his door, he wasn't surprised by the bold gesture. In the short time he'd known her, he'd quit being amazed by her take-charge attitude. Apparently, that was Caty. There was a backbone of pure steel under that sweet exterior. Strange as it seemed, he was beginning to like that about her.

Because she'd already turned to go inside, he followed after her. A curtain swished in one of the neighbors' windows, and he had to grin. He'd been here thirty seconds, and it wouldn't take much longer than that for the infamous Harland gossip chain to spread the news.

"Aren't you worried about your neighbors?" he asked when Caty stopped on the porch.

"Why?"

"Having me here this late might not be good for your reputation."

"I have a reputation for doing exactly what I want," she informed him with a sassy grin. "I don't worry much about what other folks think."

"Isn't that what got you fired?"

She thought for a second and laughed. "Yes, thank goodness. I couldn't stand that place. A bunch of people in designer suits killing themselves to make enough money to afford their Beemers and Caribbean condos. I'd rather go back to waitressing than be chained to a desk waiting for my life to start."

Matt recognized the words he'd flung at her during one of their many disputes, and he cringed. "Sorry about that. I was out of line."

"Don't apologize. You were totally right, and I'm glad you said it. Not many people have the nerve to be honest with me. They think it'll crush my fragile little heart," she added in a thick, Southern-honey accent, the back of her hand against her forehead in a melodramatic pose.

For the first time all day, he felt a genuine smile lift his spirits. "Well, then, you're welcome."

"Just don't do it again," she threatened, pointing a stern finger at him. "I'll have to retaliate."

"Yes, ma'am." He opened the new screen door for her

and stopped short when he saw the empty living room. "Where is everything?"

"Back in Grandpa's workroom. I thought I'd start painting in here. I'm thinking yellow with white trim would really brighten things up."

"Sounds nice. How'd you move everything?"

"With an old dolly, a piece at a time," she said matter-of-factly. "It took me a while."

Something wasn't right with that, but it took him a second to figure it out. "Where's the desk?"

"A couple of clerks from the hardware store moved it into the workroom for me. That's where it will end up, anyway, when my office is in there. I tried to pay them, but they wouldn't let me."

"I'm sure."

Her eyes narrowed, and she glowered up at him. "What's that supposed to mean?"

"Were you wearing that?" he asked, nodding at the cutoff denim shorts and pink tank top.

"Well, yes."

There wasn't a man alive who wouldn't help her out, dressed that way. *Cute and country,* he grumbled silently. Nobody could resist that. Then again, he reminded himself, it was none of his business.

"How's your water?" he asked, to change the subject.

She made a sick face. "Blech. Mrs. Fairman lets me grab drinking water at her house, so it's no big deal. Once it's clear, I'm gonna take a nice bubble bath."

It was impossible not to echo the smile lighting her face. "Simple pleasures, right?"

"They're the best," she agreed. "I stopped by Ruthy's for some chicken salad and coleslaw. Would you like some?"

The open, friendly invitation made him feel welcome in her house. For some reason, he was uncomfortable with that. While he enjoyed spending time with her, he really didn't want to make a habit of it. Even if he hadn't been planning to go back to Charlotte, his growing fondness for this bright, compassionate woman would have made him uneasy.

Dating women was one thing. Getting attached was something else again.

"I didn't come to eat your food," he replied, surprised at the harsh way the words came out.

Caty either didn't notice or didn't mind. Tilting her head, she looked him squarely in the eye. "Then why did you come?"

He could have made up a reason about checking her roof or something, but she'd see right through it. Out of sheer, stubborn pride, he refused to look away, even though that direct gaze made him want to squirm.

"I don't know," he admitted. "I just started driving and ended up here."

"Why?"

Her gentle tone pried under the edge of the rigid control he'd kept in place since the funeral, and he wrestled it back into place.

"I don't know," he repeated, disgusted by the quiver in his voice. "I should go."

She gave him a worried look. "Are you sure you're okay to drive?"

"Yeah, I'm fine," he lied, fishing his keys out of his pocket.

Caty closed her hand over his and gave a little squeeze. "If you want to stay, you can. You don't have to talk to me or anything."

That did it. He didn't know if it was the warmth of her touch, or the fact that he knew she understood what he was feeling, even if he didn't. A wave of indescribable emotions overwhelmed him, twisting like a knot in his chest. Rubbing a hand over his breastbone, he sat down on the stairs and waited for the sensation to die down. He'd been in pain before, but never like this.

Guilt rushed in first, swamped by regret for neglecting the only family he had. His father's image swam into his mind, his expression a combination of sadness and pride. Different as they were, Dad had accepted him as he was, applauding his strengths and accepting his flaws.

No one would ever love him like that again.

"Marianne, it's Caty." Whispering into her phone, she peeked in the kitchen window to check on Matt. She'd invented a leak under the sink to give her time to go out on the porch and make a quick call. "I just wanted you to know Matt's here."

"Oh, thank goodness. Hang on a minute." Marianne relayed the news to whoever was with her. "We didn't know he'd left until the kids starting looking for him to say goodnight."

She sounded irritated, and Caty couldn't blame her. Matt should have said something before leaving the farm. Then again, she was impressed that he'd made it through the past several days as well as he had. "Well, he's fine. Right now he's under my kitchen sink, but he should be home soon."

"Okay. Caty, I want to thank you for your help with everything. It means a lot to all of us."

"I haven't really done much, but you're welcome."

"You're doing more than you know," Marianne corrected her in a tired voice.

"Go hug your kids," Caty suggested. "And then get some sleep. I'll see you soon."

"Great idea. Good night."

"'Night."

Switching off the phone, Caty found Matt framed in the open window.

"There's nothing wrong with those pipes," he said in an accusing tone. "You were just trying to keep me busy so you could talk to my sister."

He strolled from the kitchen and through the front door, onto the porch.

"She was worried about you," Caty explained.

He grimaced. "Yeah, so was I. You're John's age, right? Twenty-eight?"

Coming out of the blue like that, the question puzzled her. "A few months younger. Why?"

"How is it somebody that young is so good at making people open up?"

She'd never really thought about it, and she shrugged. "I just wait till they're ready to start talking. Then I listen."

"Most people don't bother," he complained, looking over her shoulder at nothing in particular. "They're too busy telling you how you should feel."

"They're wrong. God made everyone different, and they handle things their own way. It's not my place to second-guess His handiwork."

Matt's aimless gaze settled on her, and he studied her with a curious expression. "You really believe all that, don't you?"

"Yes, I do."

"Even after what happened to your mom?"

Given his own experience, it would be hard for him to understand. Maybe even impossible. But she decided to give it a shot.

"God didn't take her away from me," she began, choosing her words carefully. "She chose to get into a car with a man who'd had too much to drink. If she'd called a cab, my life would've been very different. But then I wouldn't have known my grandparents as well as I did, and they're the ones who gave me what I needed to be the person I am. Including my faith," she added to be absolutely clear.

He didn't comment on that, but came back with an approving smile. "They did a great job."

"So did Ethan. He took four totally different kids and helped them grow into strong, independent people. You're all unique, but you have one important thing in common."

He gave her a skeptical look. "What's that?"

She almost answered, then thought better of it. Given enough time, she had no doubt he'd come up with it on his own. And when he did, he'd see the future—and the past—in a much more positive light.

"You're a smart guy," she challenged him with a little grin. "Figure it out for yourself."

Chapter Seven

Sunday morning dawned sunny and warm.

Outside Caty's bedroom window, a family of birds was chattering to each other, while in the background she heard the whir of her neighbor's lawn mower. It wasn't long before she caught the scent of fresh-cut grass mingled with her roses, and she took a deep breath to savor it. Back in Charlotte, Sundays had started with a frenzy of emails and phone messages she'd rushed through before going to church.

Here, she could just breathe. The difference was remarkable for its simplicity, but that didn't make it any less important. Until she was forced to resettle in Harland, she hadn't realized that she'd quite literally forgotten how to stop and smell the roses.

The shower squealed until the pipes were well primed, but the water had gone from rust-colored to just cloudy. Another couple of days, and she'd be sinking into that long-awaited bubble bath she'd mentioned to Matt.

She pulled on a pretty dress she hadn't worn in years, and it felt brand-new. Multicolored pastel flowers were sprinkled all over it, which made it easy to pick a pair of shoes. It wasn't up to the standards of dress in Boston or

Charlotte, but she'd always liked it so she'd held on to it. After some earrings and a spritz of jasmine perfume, she was ready to go. A quick spin in front of the mirror told her she was dressed perfectly for a Sunday in Harland.

It was such a beautiful morning, she decided to walk across town to the church. Along the way, she talked with several folks headed the same way. She connected with George and Priscilla Fairman in the parking lot and accepted their invitation to sit with them in their customary pew.

While chatting with the people around her, Caty soaked up the warm feeling she'd gotten the very first time she'd stepped into the little church with her grandparents. At nine years old, she was about as shy as a kid could get. Having her mother wrenched out of her life had only made things worse.

She still remembered being terrified of meeting all those strangers, even though they were friends of Gram and Grandpa. But when she walked through those doors, she wasn't scared anymore.

To this day, she knew that God had embraced that frightened, disoriented child, welcoming her to His house. Here, in this simple white church, Caty had learned that Jesus loved her and that her mother was waiting for her in Heaven. She learned that no matter how bleak things might look, she was never truly alone.

This morning the Sawyers sat in a huddle near the front, apparently receiving condolences from the people seated around them. Matt wasn't with them, of course, and while Caty wasn't surprised, she was disappointed. Just this once, would it have killed him to be with his family in church? She knew it would have meant the world to them, and in her head she scolded him for his selfishness. Maybe the bad vibes would reach him wherever he was and make him feel guilty.

The mean thought made *her* feel guilty, and she quickly amended it with something more understanding. If there was one thing she'd learned in her life, it was to be tolerant. Or at least try to be. It wasn't easy with everyone, but for those people she tried hardest. Recognizing that Matt fell into that category made her sigh. She had a lot of work ahead of her with that one. But Ethan had trusted her to help his family in his absence, and she wasn't about to let him down.

When the organist began her opening chords, Caty picked up a well-worn hymnal and stood to sing along. She loved singing, even though she couldn't accurately hit most of the notes. On a morning like this, she really didn't care. Surrounded by good, honest folks who still took the time to slow down on Sundays made her feel more light-hearted than she had in a long time.

Once everyone sat back down, Pastor Charles let his gaze drift over the congregation until it settled on her. He gave her a dimpled smile and a quick wink of warning.

"This morning, I'd like to welcome home one of Harland's favorite daughters, Caty Lee McKenzie." People quietly applauded, and she smiled in response. "I'd like to encourage old friends and new to offer her your good wishes, and keep her in mind when you find yourself needing a lawyer."

Very appropriately, his uplifting sermon about hope matched the weather, and Caty ended the final hymn feeling as though she could take on the world. Which was a good thing, because she had a lot of tedious work to do.

Outside, she waited for the Sawyers to work their way through what amounted to a receiving line of hugs and offers of help. By the time they got to her, the kids were impatient and the grown-ups looked a little overwhelmed.

"Can we go on the swings, Mommy?" Emily asked, pointing across the lawn at the playground.

"No, honey. We all start school this week, and we have a lot to do at home."

Kyle's hopeful look drooped into a frown, but to his credit he didn't say anything. It was obvious Marianne hated to disappoint them, and Caty jumped in.

"I can take them, Mare. Just leave me Emily's car seat, and I'll bring them home after lunch."

Kyle's eyes lit up like the boy he was. "Can we put the top down on your car?"

"Yes," she replied, ruffling his sun-streaked brown hair. "I'll even show you how to do it."

"Are you sure?" Marianne asked. "Aren't you busy with your house?"

Caty waved that away, grateful for an excuse to put it off. She really could use a break. "None of those jobs are going anywhere, believe me. They'll wait till tomorrow."

"We could help you!" Emily offered, blue eyes shining with excitement. "I like cleaning."

Caty was amazed. She couldn't imagine many four-year-olds actually enjoyed housework. "Really? Why?"

"Things look so nice when you're done."

"I appreciate the offer, Emmy, but I was thinking more like, play here awhile and then have lunch at Ruthy's. I know she'd be thrilled to see you two."

"We love Ruthy." Kyle's bright grin reminded her of John's. "She always gives us extra fries so they won't spoil."

That sounded like her, and Caty said, "When I was little, she'd let me scoop my own ice cream. Maybe if we ask real nice, she'll let us do that today."

"Cool," he approved. "Can we sit at the counter?"

Caty laughed. "I used to love that, too. My grandpa would spin me on the stool till I got dizzy."

"Then you have to go the other way," Emily informed her in a serious voice. "Falling off a stool is no fun."

"Very true," Caty agreed, holding out a hand for each of them. "Shall we?"

They both hugged their mother and then took her hands. After a quick debate, they decided to run in zigzags the whole way out to the playground.

While she pushed Emily on a swing, Caty asked her if she was excited about school.

"Yes," the little girl answered with a bright smile. "My friend Jenny's in my class. We're going to sit together."

"That sounds great."

After a few more pushes, out of nowhere Emily asked, "Did you come here with your daddy to play when you were little?"

"No," Caty managed around the sudden lump in her throat. "I didn't see him when I was growing up."

"Me, neither. It makes my mommy sad. Did it make your mommy sad?"

Honestly, Caty recalled nothing but bitter silence. Mom had been furious with him, but Caty had never understood what had driven them apart. Maybe the situation *had* made her mother sad, but she hadn't wanted to show it.

Caty didn't know how to explain all that to Emily, so she asked, "What are you wearing the first day of school?"

That set off a much more pleasant conversation, and Caty tucked unanswered questions about her father back into the past where they belonged.

Matt didn't remember them having all this equipment. John had filled him in on their recent purchases, including a monstrous baler for the huge, round bales many farmers preferred for livestock. It wasn't brand-new, but he didn't want to think about how much it had cost. They still sold the smaller square bales to many local farms, but for dairy farmers with a hundred cows or more, it was a lot easier to drop a round bale in the pasture and let them eat it down to nothing. To keep up with the competition, you had to give your customers what they wanted, and that meant having the latest tools.

John was out with the baler now, finishing up the largest hayfield by headlights. Matt was slowly discovering that preventive maintenance around the farm had fallen by the wayside, and just about everything mechanical needed something or other. Oil changes, spark plugs, general cleaning and lubing. Then there were belts to replace, gears to grease, and a few more major repairs.

It was a lot of work, but he found himself enjoying it. While he was growing up, he'd spent countless hours here in the workshop with his father, learning how to diagnose all kinds of mechanical problems and fix them. John loved working outside all day, but for Matt it was more like torture. Farming was a never-ending proposition. At least in here, he felt a sense of accomplishment when he fixed something and it ran right.

Until the next piece of equipment broke, and he started all over again.

Dad's toolbox wasn't exactly organized, and Matt wasted a good bit of time hunting for the right-size wrench or socket for each job. Finally, he decided he could save his sanity if he took a break and arranged each piece by size. When he came up three sockets short, he groaned. He needed one of them to finish his current job.

A hopeless pack rat, Dad had always prided himself on never losing anything, even if he might not have been able to find it right away. Hands on his hips, Matt looked around for odd places those sockets could be. Chances were they'd ended up in Dad's pocket and dropped out somewhere while he was working. Matt found one of them under a nearby stool, and another holding up the short leg of an old workbench.

Sighing, Matt retrieved the socket and hunted for a block of wood to take its place. As he slid it under the short leg, the floorboard beneath it rocked with a disheartening thunk. He groaned again, louder this time. He had enough to do without having to batten the old floorboards down.

Then again, he'd be in this workshop a lot over the next few weeks. One loose floorboard usually meant there were more, and he didn't want to kill himself stumbling over anything. His sentence at the farm would be tough enough if he was healthy. He didn't want to think about how hard it would be if he wrenched his back or twisted an ankle.

So he got a hammer and a jelly jar full of nails and started testing the boards. The loose ones were all in the same area, which seemed odd. Lifting the first one, he found a rectangular metal box in the hollow space. It had a padlock on it, and he wondered why. He shook it but heard only the rustle of paper. Another board, another box. By the time he was done, he had five of them, all the same size and apparently full of paper.

They were labeled, one for each of the last five years. More than a little intrigued, he lined them up on the workbench to get a better look at them. Folding his arms, he stared at them and wondered what on earth his father had been hiding out here. They must be important, because he'd gone to the trouble of putting them in metal boxes to protect them from mice.

The padlocks were no problem. Matt took a crowbar off the peg rack and pried the locks open easily enough. As he sifted through the contents, his excitement dimmed, and his heart sank a little more with each lid he opened.

There, under the fluorescent lights, sat his worst nightmare.

"Hey, there." When Caty answered Matt's call, she was holding a pile of yellow color swatches in one hand and another pile of white in the other. "What's up?"

"You busy?"

Matt was never tactful, but he sounded even more terse than usual. "Not really. Why?"

"I need to talk to you."

The tension in his voice reached through the grainy connection, and she put the swatches down to give him her full attention. "Go ahead."

"I know it's late, but can we do this in person?"

"Sure. I'll be there in—"

"No!" Sighing, he amended his order. "Sorry about that. Can I come to your place?"

"Of course. Matt, what's wrong?"

"Everything."

That was her only hint before he hung up. Even more worried now, she wondered if his problem had something to do with Ethan's estate. Or the farm. Had some developer made him an outrageous offer? While she waited for him to arrive, she ran various scenarios through her head so she'd be ready for whatever he had to say.

Not even her vivid imagination could have prepared her for the truth.

"Say that again," she said very deliberately, eyeing the metal boxes Matt had brought with him.

"The farm's bankrupt," he replied grimly, jaw clenched against the harshness of his words. "It's been headed that way for a while now, and Dad was up to his neck in debt trying to save it."

His eyes were a stormy gray, and they narrowed as they lasered in on her. After a few seconds of that, he snarled, "Did you know?"

"No."

It was the simple, honest truth, and it made her sick. As Ethan's attorney, she should have been aware of the situation, but he never gave her any indication there was a problem. Judging by the way Matt had found out, he hadn't told anyone. "Does your family know?"

"I don't think so. He hid all this in his workshop. John's all over the farm, but even he doesn't go in there." Setting the boxes on the steps, Matt sank down beside them. "What I don't get is how he kept it from Marianne. She's the farm's bookkeeper."

"I don't know." Caty was just as baffled as he was. "Maybe the answer's in these boxes somewhere. The light's best in the kitchen. Let's take them in there and spread everything out. If we organize it chronologically, maybe we can figure out what's been going on."

"I'm not sure I want to know."

The growl in his voice warned her he was dangerously close to the edge. Forcing a smile, she picked up two of the boxes in an effort to make him feel as though she'd lightened his load a bit. "I'm Ethan's executor, so technically this is my job. Why don't you go on home? I'll call you when I figure it out."

She expected him to bolt, or at least take a minute to consider her offer. Instead, he surprised her with, "Have any sweet tea?"

"In the fridge," she said as she went into the kitchen. "Help yourself."

He followed her and helped her arrange the boxes in

order on the counter. Pulling down the old-fashioned lever to open the fridge, he said, "This thing still works?"

"Off and on. I wouldn't put food in there, but it's fine for drinks. Gus is ordering a new one and letting me have it wholesale."

Matt swallowed some tea. "In return for?"

"He wants to buy the building next to the hardware store and expand. I told him I'd handle the closing for him."

Some of the tension left his face, and Matt chuckled as he sat down on the tall stool that was currently her only seating. "Sounds like Gus."

"He's saving me six hundred and fifteen dollars," Caty commented as she sorted Ethan's paperwork into piles on the counter. "Works for me."

After that, the only noise in the house was shuffling papers and the soft tick of the grandfather clock. With each box she sorted, Caty's usual optimism faded a little more. Elbows on the counter, Matt folded his hands and rested his chin on them. While she worked, she felt him watching her, but he didn't say a word.

When she was done, she stood back, folded her arms and frowned.

"Yeah," he muttered, "that's what I came up with, too."

"How on earth did this happen?" she asked, knowing Matt had probably already asked himself that. "The farm's been failing for the past five years."

"Knowing Dad, it was in trouble before that," Matt said with a sigh. "That new baler cost a small fortune, and last year's bills for maintenance were close to six figures. They're not as much this year, but stuff's been breaking down left and right."

"He was neglecting the maintenance to save money," she said to show she understood.

Matt nodded curtly. "The other problem is income. Crop

prices go up and down every year, mostly down, but he always trusted things would work out for the best."

Caty heard what he wasn't saying and called him on it. "Trusted God, you mean."

"Whatever." Scowling, he spread his hands over the mess. "What can I do?"

Being male, and a mechanic to boot, Matt struck her as the kind of person who was used to assessing a problem and then fixing it. Unfortunately, it would take more than his considerable will to resolve this one.

Hoping to keep him focused on things they could actually do something about, she started with a simple one. "I don't have any documentation on these loans or this checking account. He opened it online, so it could be based anywhere."

"Makes sense he wouldn't do it around here. People would know, and then they'd start talking."

"No doubt about it, he was covering his tracks. The account number and codes are right here, so I should be able to find out what's going on." She picked up the most recent statement. "But there's a balance of fourteen dollars. Judging by this, he deposited his paycheck every other week and immediately wrote out a check for the same amount." She picked up another statement. "One check paid the installment on the baler, the other went to the loan."

"A huge personal loan with a ridiculous interest rate," Matt added gloomily. "And that's not the first one he took out. I don't get it. If they needed money so bad, why didn't he just mortgage the farm?"

Caty thought that one over, because he was right. It didn't make sense. Considering what she knew about Ethan and the changes he'd recently made to his will, she came up with a logical explanation.

"I think he wanted to pass along the farm free and clear,

Inspirational Romance Reading...

Rocky Point Promise
Barbara McMahon

TWO BOOKS FREE!

Each of your FREE books feature contemporary love stories that will lift your spirits and reinforce important lessons about life, faith and love.

We'd like to send you two free books to introduce you to the Reader Service. Your two books have a combined cover price of $11.50 for the regular-print or $13.00 for the larger-print in the U.S. and $13.50 for the regular-print or $15.00 for the larger-print in Canada, but they are yours free! We'll even send you two exciting surprise gifts. There's no catch. You're under no obligation to buy anything. We charge nothing– ZERO – for your first shipment. *You can't lose!*

Visit us at
www.ReaderService.com

YOURS FREE!

We'll send you 2 fabulous surprise gifts (worth about $10) just for trying "Inspirational Romance"!

The Reader Service — Here's How it Works:

in case something happened to him. Then you could sell it, pay off the debts, and Marianne and John would still have their houses to live in. For the rest of you, the life insurance would be your inheritance."

"Forget about paying it off," Matt grumbled. "Until we start getting some harvest income, we can't make the regular payments. Even if we hauled everything in tomorrow, we wouldn't get paid for at least a month."

Caty glanced at the terms printed at the bottom of the loan contract. "The penalty for missing a payment is atrocious. The way things are with the economy right now, the bank might even call in the loan."

Muttering under his breath, Matt swung himself off the stool and stalked to the window. Hands shoved into the back pockets of his oil-stained jeans, he glared out at the town with a disgust she could almost feel. "What should I do?"

Sensing he didn't really want pragmatism right now, she asked, "What do you want to do?"

"Sell the place and go home. It's a great spot, and two developers have called me already. They offered me way more than enough to pay everything off."

"You can do that. I'm sure once you explain what's going on, John and the girls will understand."

She used a soothing tone to calm him down, so that he'd realize he really didn't want to do that at all. She hoped. This was the kind of thing that looked good on paper, but when the bulldozers and construction crews showed up, people often regretted their decision.

"No." Turning to face her, his expression took on a different quality. Not softer, exactly, but not quite so furious. "I can't tell them about this debt."

Completely stunned, it took her a few seconds to come

up with something reasonable to say. All she could manage was a very lame, "You have to."

"The father they just buried has been lying to them for years," he reminded her curtly. "You really think they want to hear that right now?"

"Protecting them," she corrected, moving to stand in front of him. "Whenever he could, he made extra payments on the loan. To me, that says he was confident he could pay it off and avoid worrying them."

"You think if I tell them now, they won't worry?"

She sensed that she was losing this argument, and she searched for a way to shock him into seeing reason. "If you don't, they'll think selling the farm was all your decision, and they'll hate you."

"That's better than them hating Dad."

"They still have a right to know. This is your family's legacy you're talking about," she added, hoping the reference to the Sawyers' history would get through his thick, stubborn skull.

He just folded his massive arms and stared back at her. Refusing to let him get away with that, she tried switching tactics.

"Based on the conversation we had about Ethan's will, I think the girls would agree to sell," she said, taking a sip from the open water bottle she'd left by the sink. "But what about John?"

"He'll still have a place to live, and everyone knows what a hard worker he is. He could have a job at any farm within ten miles."

Using a courtroom tactic she'd learned in law school, Caty waited patiently for Matt to look at her. When his eyes met hers, very quietly she said, "He's happy working his family's farm. It means everything to him." After considering how far to push him, she decided to go for broke.

"And you know it."

Anger blazed in Matt's eyes, and then the brilliant blue darkened to an ominous slate color. Hard, unbending, it was more intimidating than the fury she'd seen a few seconds ago. But she was right, so she held her ground, refusing to look away, even though her tired, gritty eyes really needed to blink.

After what felt like forever, his anger receded just a little, the rigidity giving way to something resembling respect.

"I'll think about it," he finally said, the grinding tone telling her it wasn't easy for him.

Caty wasn't accustomed to losing arguments, but she knew that she'd win this one only if Matt gave in. That didn't seem likely right now. Once he thought it through, he just might make the right choice. Then again, this was a guy who'd avoided everything related to Harland for the past fifteen years. The precarious financial situation at the farm was his out. She prayed he wouldn't take it.

Keeping her voice even, Caty opted for a very professional response. "I'll call the bank tomorrow and start the process for getting this checking account closed."

"Okay." Fishing his keys out of his pocket, Matt glanced at the papers stacked on her counter. "Can I leave those with you?"

"Sure," she agreed as she walked him to the front door. "I've got a fireproof cabinet for all my legal work. I'll put everything in there and keep it safe for you."

"Thanks."

Being so clinical about everything simply wasn't her style, so she dropped the act. "Matt, I'm so sorry. You have so much to deal with already, this must feel like another weight on your shoulders."

"It doesn't help, that's for sure."

Her heart went out to him, and she couldn't keep her distance anymore. Resting a hand on his windburned cheek, she summoned her most encouraging smile. "I know it seems unbearable right now, but promise me you'll sleep on it before you make a decision."

Closing his eyes as though he was in terrible pain, he covered her hand with his and sighed. "Okay."

Satisfied for now, she stepped back and gave him his space. He left her with a halfhearted smile and trudged down the steps. Shoulders slumped, he climbed into his truck and stared out the windshield into the darkness beyond the lone streetlight. When he started the engine, the interior lights threw shadows over his miserable expression. As he drove down the street, she wished there was something she could do for him.

Matt had always been strong and confident, to the point of arrogance. Better-looking than any guy had a right to be, he used that rugged charm of his to his best advantage. He towered over everyone, secure in his cocky assessment of the world around him.

With everything he'd had to manage since his father's death, tonight was the first time Caty had seen him look defeated.

Chapter Eight

Monday morning dawned early, but all the Sawyers gathered around the kitchen table for breakfast while the kids were still asleep. After a bracing swallow of Marianne's high-octane coffee, Matt told John and the girls what he'd discovered last night. Then he sat back and looked at each of them, trying to gauge the impact of what he'd said. Although he'd spent a restless night going through the options, he still hadn't made up his mind about what to do. He was counting on their reactions to help him make the toughest decision of his life.

At first, all he got was dead silence. The three of them traded pained looks, obviously trying to come to terms with what he'd said.

As he'd expected, Marianne spoke first. She was the self-appointed mother hen of the family, always practical when it came to the farm. "I don't understand. I do the books, and I had no idea. I mean, things are tight, but that's nothing new. How could he manage to do something like this?"

"He used his salary to make the payments on the loans. From what Caty and I saw, he didn't make a dime the last five years."

Frowning, Lisa asked, "Do you think the stress from all these financial problems caused his heart attack?"

Matt hadn't considered that, but it would make sense. Their father was one for keeping bad things to himself to avoid worrying the rest of them. Keeping all that bottled up couldn't be healthy.

It made him appreciate the fact that for the first time he could remember, he had someone to take some of the load off him. He knew he could trust Caty to handle the banks, while he walked his family through the mess their father had left behind.

Because they were all still shaken by the whole thing, Matt kept it vague. "We won't ever know that, I guess. The question is, what do we do now?"

"Are we gonna lose the farm?" John asked very quietly.

"Not in this lifetime," Matt promised him with more confidence than he felt. The irony of it didn't escape him. Just last night, he'd pretty much told Caty he was ready to sell the place and take off. He wasn't sure what had happened, but during the night, something had changed.

"If you, John and I pool the money Dad left us, we could pay off most of the debt," Lisa suggested. "The kids would still have theirs."

"You can have mine," John agreed quickly. "I don't really need it for anything."

"I thought of that, too, but we won't get that money until next year." Still, their willingness to share the pain took some of the burden off him, and he smiled proudly at them. "I appreciate the offer, though."

"We might need it later," John pointed out. "I won't buy that Ferrari I've had my eye on, just in case," he added with a grin.

Grateful to him for easing the tension, Matt couldn't help grinning back. "Good idea. I was thinking about that new baler last night. If we sell it, we could make a dent. How many people buy those huge, round bales?"

John made a list of the customers by name, ticking them off on his fingers. When he ran out of fingers, Matt stopped him.

"That's too many," he decided, biting back a sigh. "We need to give folks what they want or they'll get their hay from somebody else."

"That's the last thing we need," John commented with a frown.

Matt hated to see the worry in his carefree little brother's eyes, but there was no help for it. They were all in this together, so everybody had to know what they were up against.

"This is going to take a lot longer than you planned," Marianne pointed out. "Maybe you should get back to Charlotte and let us work it out here."

"I thought of that, actually. I could take on some extra projects for spare cash. Then I could send money back here to keep things going until the harvest money comes in." She opened her mouth to say something, and he added, "But I'm not gonna leave this mess for John. With Caty's help, we'll figure something out."

"Caty will know what to do," Lisa agreed. "She always does."

He didn't want to admit he'd gone to Caty first, so he said, "That's good to hear. I'll talk to her later today."

The difficult conversation had gone better than he'd expected. He just hoped they'd feel as optimistic when the money ran out.

Around noon, Caty's phone rang. She was in the middle of scraping flaking paint off the windowsills, but she put down her scraper and checked the caller ID. To her surprise, it was Matt. She'd spoken to him not half an hour ago to tell him the bank had agreed to keep the loan in place. Where they'd get the money was another issue, but unfortunately she couldn't help him with that.

"Talk to me," he pleaded when she answered. "I'm going crazy out here."

"Where is here?"

"Tractor supply. They're mounting a new tire, and it's taking forever. I even offered to go back and do it myself, but the snail running this place won't let me. I had to come out to my truck to keep from strangling him."

She chuckled. "Good choice. I couldn't do much about a murder rap, I'm afraid."

"It'd be self-defense. Defending my sanity."

"Did anyone ever tell you you've got a dark sense of humor?"

This time, he chuckled. "My friends usually don't get my jokes."

"Sarcasm is lost on most people."

"Got that right. So what are you doing?"

"Scraping paint. It's almost as stimulating as watching it dry, but not quite."

"My sympathies." The background noise muffled, and he came back on. "My tire's finally done, so I have to go. Talk to you later."

He hung up before she could say anything else. Why had he called her? They hardly knew each other, and she couldn't imagine why he'd think of her when he was bored. It was thoughtful, she supposed, but it seemed completely out of character. Matt didn't strike her as the type to call anyone just to chat.

Baffled by the whole thing, she returned to the window. She came across a stubborn patch of paint that looked as though it was covering some kind of putty. Digging out the goop would damage the wood, and she kicked herself for not thinking to buy paint thinner. She'd been to the hardware store three times today, but it hadn't occurred to her.

After adding paint thinner to her list, Caty wandered into her grandfather's workroom, thinking she might find some in one of the mystery bottles she'd noticed in there. If so, it would be old, but it might be strong enough to soften the wood filler, so that she could remove it without damaging the trim. She angled her way through the furniture and stacked boxes to get to the shelves.

Squinting to read the faded labels, she found all manner of liquids for various purposes. Some were Grandpa's own concoctions, which he'd insisted worked better than the commercial variety. A wooden box near the back caught her attention. She remembered him keeping different kinds of paints and glues in it, organized just as neatly as Gram's sewing kit. There might be something in there she could use.

Like the rest of the house, nothing had changed since he last touched it. When she lifted the lid, the upper tray hinged up and out, and she found a small bottle of mineral spirits still upright in the bottom.

"This should do the trick," she said aloud. She really needed to get a cat or something. This talking to herself was starting to worry her.

She was about to close the lid when she noticed the corner of an envelope under some old cotton pads. She dug it out and was surprised to see her name on it. How long had it been in here? And why on earth had he hidden it away?

Feeling like Nancy Drew, Caty took the envelope into the kitchen where the light was better. It was addressed to her, care of her grandfather, and the return address was a post office box in Raleigh. Strangely, the postmark was more than twenty years old.

Stranger still, the letter had never been opened.

A shiver of excitement danced up her back as she opened the flap. She took out a sheet of paper, wrapped around a picture of a slender young man holding a baby. Dated just after her first birthday, the page was filled on both sides with small, precise handwriting.

It began, "My darling daughter."

Caty was so stunned, she didn't realize she'd dropped everything until the pieces fluttered to the floor. She wasn't even sure she wanted to read any more. Shaking with disbelief, she sat down and took the picture by the corners to avoid smudging the only image she'd ever seen of her father.

Dressed in khaki pants and a green polo shirt, he was tall, with wavy brown hair tinged with red, like hers. She couldn't see his eyes because he was looking down at the pink blanket cradled in his arms. But in the delighted smile on his face she saw pure, shining love. The sight brought on more tears than she could blink away, and she put the picture down to keep it dry.

Her father had loved her.

The sudden knowledge hit her hard, and she didn't bother trying to stem the tears. During a rare conversation about him, her mother had told her he took off long before Caty was born, unable to face the responsibilities of being a father.

For years, Mom had repeatedly lied to her about the whole thing. But why?

Hoping to find the answer, Caty dried her eyes on the relatively clean sleeve of her grimy T-shirt, and picked up the letter.

"I'm sending this to your grandfather because he's a

good man, and I trust him to make sure you get it when you're ready. I only wish I could deliver it in person so I could see you again. I think about you every day, wondering what you're doing and if maybe you still look like me."

Caty swallowed hard around the lump in her throat, but kept reading. He told her about himself, where he was raised, where he worked, that he and his parents lived in Raleigh. He traveled a lot as a sales rep for a company that, Caty knew, had gone out of business ten years ago. He loved her, her mother and the Atlanta Braves, in that order. He had a sweet tooth but hated spicy food. The list continued on the back page, and she drank in every detail.

Every time her mother had lamented how different she and Caty were, she was indirectly criticizing this man. He didn't give his name until the end.

There's not much else to tell. I hope one day you'll understand that I love you with all my heart and wish I could be part of your life. I don't blame your mother for leaving, and neither should you. She did what she thought was best for both of you. We simply weren't meant to be a family, but I dearly love my little girl, and I will never forget you.

Your father, Brian Jameson.

The last few words blurred in a haze of tears, and she finally broke down. Sobbing uncontrollably into her hands, she was more than sad. She was furious at her mother for keeping her from knowing Brian Jameson. Instead, she'd taught Caty that when things got tough, men simply left. It was in their nature, she'd said time and again. They could leave, so they did. It colored every meaningful relationship Caty had ever tried to have. Finally, after David had left her for someone else, she'd given up on the idea of finding someone to share her life with.

How different would things have been if Caty had known that her father hadn't selfishly abandoned her, but had in fact wanted them to be a family? If he'd been in their lives, her mother wouldn't have needed a ride home the night she died. She'd have called Brian, and he would have gotten her home safely. Caty would have had a normal life with two parents, rather than the patchwork childhood her grandparents had stitched together for her.

Consumed by anger and bitterness, she didn't know how long she sat there like that. Just when she thought the powerful emotions were receding, another wave hit her and knocked her back down.

From out of nowhere, a pair of strong arms came around her, and she leaned into them, even though she wasn't completely sure who they belonged to.

"Caty, what is it?" Matt asked, his deep voice filled with concern. "What's wrong?"

"She lied to me," she snarled. "All my life, she lied."

"Who did?"

"My mother." She still couldn't believe it, and saying it made her cry harder.

"Why?"

"I don't know," she sobbed.

Without pulling away, she held up her father's letter. While Matt read, she kept crying because she didn't know how to stop.

"He didn't leave," she moaned on a ragged breath. "He loved me."

Stroking her back with a comforting hand, Matt murmured, "Of course he did. Who wouldn't love a cute little thing like you?"

The humor got through to her, and Caty managed something between a hiccup and a laugh. She drew her head back and absentmindedly lifted her hands to wipe her eyes.

"Don't do that," Matt chided. "Your hands are filthy." He grabbed a paper towel from the roll on the counter and handed it to her.

After a few false starts, she finally calmed down and took a deep breath. Looking up, she forced a smile to get the stricken look off his face. "Thanks, Matt."

"You're welcome." Picking up the envelope, he frowned. "Where'd you find this?"

"In one of Grandpa's boxes."

"Why didn't he give it to you?"

She shrugged. "Gram hated my father, so maybe Grandpa was afraid it would make her mad. After she died, maybe he forgot, or he thought it didn't matter anymore."

But it did.

Caty thought she'd come to terms with the whole thing, but her father's revelation brought it all to the surface in vivid, painful color. She'd missed so much with him—an entire lifetime—because her mother had decided she hated someone she'd once loved.

Matt brushed a stray lock of hair back from her damp cheek. "I guess you'll never know."

She sighed. "Maybe it's better that way. If she was here right now, I'd ream her out for pulling this."

Chuckling, Matt hugged her a little closer. Normally she hated being coddled, but his hold was comforting without strangling her. It felt so good, she wanted to burrow into it and stay.

Then her brain intruded, warning her that she was treading in very dangerous territory. Matt Sawyer wasn't a man to get attached to. He was a wanderer who made no bones about returning to his old life the first chance he got. He wasn't interested in settling down anywhere, and especially not in Harland. Now that she was so happily settled back at home, she never wanted to live anyplace else.

Being snuggled in his arms felt wonderful, but it wasn't right. Very reluctantly, she untangled herself and stood.

"What brings you by?" she asked.

He shrugged. "I was on my way back to the farm and wanted to see how things were going here."

"Stalling because you have a zillion things to do when you get there," she teased, hoping she sounded more normal.

"That, too." Cocking his head, he gave her a don't-lie-to-me look. "You sure you're okay?"

Nodding, she felt a sudden rush of gratitude toward this baffling man. Most of the time, he was cool and distant, but she'd seen glimpses of honest emotion beneath that controlled exterior. Maybe, she thought, his heart was warmer than the rest of him.

For some strange reason, he had opened up to her, confided in her. It had encouraged her to do the same with him. A small voice in her head whispered that he might even care about her. But that really didn't matter, did it? Even if she let him close enough to find out for sure, everything would crumble when he eventually returned to the life he enjoyed so much.

Giving her an indulgent smile and a kiss on the cheek, he strolled from the kitchen and out the front door. As she watched him walk out to his truck, the warmth she'd felt toward him kicked up a few notches.

He was a good guy, she decided, just not the right one for her. She preferred relationships to dating, while he'd made it clear he felt the opposite. Even if by some stroke of insanity he wanted to get serious, her disastrous experience with David had taught her to be very careful with her heart. The prospect of giving it to Matt was only slightly less terrifying than jumping out of an airplane with no parachute.

God had given her a brain because He wanted her to use it. And only a fool played with fire.

Matt's whirlwind trip to Charlotte ended with a half-full truck bed and a rented trailer to transport his motorcycle. Glancing into the rearview, he checked the tie-downs on the tarp he'd stretched over his load.

His apartment had been furnished, so he didn't have much. Not nearly enough for someone his age, he mused with a frown at his reflection. Most of his friends had been married at least once, and many of them had kids. He had his set of mechanic's tools, a collection of well-worn clothes, one suit and a bike. Not usually one to ponder life and the future, he couldn't help wondering where exactly he was headed.

His boss had agreed to take over Matt's current projects and keep a spot for him until November, but couldn't guarantee anything beyond that. The man had a business to run, and Matt appreciated being given time to sort things out in Harland. Of course, he had no clue how long that would take, or even how it would turn out. It was entirely possible he'd be at the farm until the end of the year and then move someplace else after that.

The idea of starting fresh usually appealed to him. This time, not so much. What was different? he wondered as he passed the sign welcoming him to Harland. He'd driven through town to the other side before he realized something was different.

Usually the sight of that sign gave him a clenching feeling in his chest. This time, it never materialized. Confused, he poked around in his head a little, but he couldn't find it.

Imagining Marianne waiting on him to unpack didn't do it. Picturing acre after acre of standing wheat didn't do it.

Then, all on its own, in floated an image of Caty, green eyes sparkling while she smiled up at him. He wasn't sure how she related to what he'd been mulling over, but he was smiling when he pulled in at the farm.

"Whoa!" Kyle flew down the back steps and climbed onto one of the trailer's rear wheels. "Is this a Harley?"

"Sure is."

"Awesome," Kyle approved as Marianne appeared on the porch. "It looks brand-new. Do you ever ride it?"

"I ride it a lot." Matt lowered the tailgate and released the wheel tethers. "But I take real good care of it."

"Could I go out with you sometime? With a helmet," he added, excitement shining in his hazel eyes.

She didn't say anything, but from where he was standing Matt sensed his sister tensing up. Grinning, he rumpled his nephew's hair the way he used to do with John. "This kind of bike is for grown-ups. When you're eighteen, we'll talk."

"That's forever."

"Only feels like it." The poor kid looked so disappointed, Matt decided to toss him a bone. "In the meantime, we can work on it together so when you're older you'll know all about it."

Matt was happy to see the boy's face light up. "That would be cool. Thanks!"

"No problem."

Kyle scampered off with Tucker, and Marianne came down from the porch with a grateful smile.

"Thanks, Matt. You made his day."

"No problem," Matt repeated as he walked the bike down the ramps. "He's fantastic, Mare. You're doing real well with him."

She looked so amazed, he glanced around to see what had gotten her attention. When nothing obvious surfaced, he figured her reaction had something to do with him. "What?"

"I think you just complimented me."

"Guess I did," he replied, a little surprised himself. Stubborn as they were, they butted heads more often than not. "You deserve it, though. Kids are tough, and you're doing a great job."

Still looking bewildered, she smiled back. "Thank you."

"You're welcome. I'll put my bike away and then come see whatever it is you want to show me."

"How did you know?"

"When a lady meets you in the driveway, she's got something to show off. Fact of life."

Giving him one of her exasperated-mom looks, she shook her head. "You're so jaded."

"Maybe," he said as he pushed the Harley past her, "but I'm right."

After parking his bike, he made sure he had the key and tossed a paint-spattered tarp over the motorcycle. He wouldn't get much time to ride it, but paying to store it in Charlotte would have been stupid when he had a perfectly good barn here to keep it in.

Just inside the kitchen door, he could hear his sisters' excited voices upstairs. He found them in their father's old room, which looked completely different.

The walls had a fresh coat of paint that was probably called Sandy Beach, or some such thing. All the trim was now a crisp white, which made a nice frame for the trees outside. New blue-and-maroon plaid curtains waved in the breeze, and the windows were spotless. Only the dresser and an armchair remained, leaving plenty of space for his king-size bed.

"You didn't have to do this," he said, not sure he liked the idea of taking over this space.

"John told us you two fight all the time, just like always," Lisa informed him. "Marianne and I thought this would help keep the peace."

"It could've waited."

"Things are getting busy at school, and pretty soon I won't have time to breathe," Marianne replied. "It was now or never."

Pushing aside his misgivings, Matt decided the change made sense. "It looks real nice. How'd you get it done so fast?"

"Caty helped," Lisa explained.

Of course she did, he thought with a grin. "Let me guess. She picked the colors."

"How could you possibly know that?" Marianne demanded.

"Her style."

Giving him an odd look, Lisa chimed in. "And how do you know *that*?"

"That's the way she's doing her living room," he explained, "so I figured she likes that kinda thing."

"You've been there?" Marianne pressed. "When?"

He'd actually been there a few times, but to anyone who didn't understand the circumstances surrounding their quick friendship, it might sound strange. Now that he thought about it, if one of his buddies was the guy in question, Matt would think it was strange, too.

To avoid the third degree, he kept his answer vague. "I helped her move some things around, is all. Speaking of which, I should unload my stuff. I want to get the rest of our equipment squared away."

"We'll help," Lisa offered, linking her arm through his as they went down the stairs. "This might sound weird, but I'm really glad you're home. I've missed having you around."

Sweet as it was, her comment made absolutely no sense to him. "I've been gone fifteen years."

"I know," she said, hugging his arm. "And I missed you all that time."

Over her head, he traded a look with Marianne, who shrugged. While he'd been wandering from place to place, he'd never considered that someone would miss him. Life on the farm went on day after day, driven by the seasons.

At first, he had kept in touch so his family—especially Dad—wouldn't feel neglected. Gradually his phone calls were spaced further apart, his visits even more so. It wasn't that he didn't care, but the conversations were all pretty much the same, because things in Harland never changed.

Until now. Matt wished for the hundredth time that his father had confided in him. Matt could have sent money, taken over some of the work his family had been paying outrageous mechanics' rates for. He could have done something, but he never got the chance.

The miles of alone time during his trip had given him a lot of time to think. With only himself for company, he'd realized he'd drifted too far away from his family. Not just in miles, but in attitude. Even though they needed him, he'd made it impossible for them to ask for his help. It was a selfish, hurtful thing to do, and he'd regret it the rest of his life.

Chapter Nine

Late one September evening, Caty slid her paint roller over the last bare patch of repaired plaster. It had taken her the better part of three days to fill in holes, sand the patches and coat the walls in the primer Gus had said she needed. Then, thanks to a timely early autumn breeze, this morning it had been dry enough to paint.

Buttercreme, the can was labeled. Somewhere between Sunny Daze and Buttercup, it was a soft yellow with a mellowing hint of cream. While she'd ridiculed the poetic names listed on the paint samples, she had to admit the designer had nailed this one perfectly.

Carefully resting the paint-covered roller in its pan, she turned to the nearly dry wall to admire her work. Since she wasn't exactly Michelangelo, there were some flaws in the plaster, but overall she was happy. Once she hung pictures over the worst spots, she'd never notice them. Unfortunately, thinking about covering flaws led her bored mind to what had become its favorite subject.

Her father's letter.

She'd read it at least a dozen times, and the memory of it made her want to smile and frown at the same time. What should she do about it? In these days of internet searches, finding him probably wouldn't be that hard. Jameson wasn't a very common name, and she knew that he was from Raleigh and the name of the company he'd worked for.

Then again, did she want to find him? Judging by his appearance in the photo, today he'd be in his fifties, probably married with a family of his own. Had he thought about her after writing that letter so long ago, or had he moved on with his life? He'd loved her as a baby wrapped in a pink blanket. Would he be proud of the woman she'd become, welcoming her into his home for a reunion? Or would he be stiffly polite, embarrassed by her unexpected appearance in his nice, orderly life?

He might even resent being forced to admit to his family that as a young man he'd fathered a child with a woman he'd never married. Now that she'd absorbed the shock of her mother's deception, Caty was trying very hard to understand and forgive. She wouldn't mind talking the whole thing over with someone, but the only other person who knew the truth was Matt.

She hadn't heard a thing from him since his trip to Charlotte. She could have invented a reason to call him, such as a question about the estate, but her pride kept her from doing that. She didn't want to pester him when he was so busy, and she certainly didn't want to give him the impression she was chasing after him the way so many women did. Especially when it was entirely possible that, while he was in Charlotte, he'd met up with some Bambi who interested him more than an unemployed attorney covered in paint and plaster dust.

"Get a grip, Caty," she scolded herself as she pounded the top back on a half-full can. "It really doesn't matter."

But it did. She knew that because she'd checked her voice mail several times a day since he'd left, and she hadn't heard his voice once. The whole thing made her sick because she wasn't that kind of girl. She'd never waited by the phone, desperate for male attention. Well, there was that mechanical engineer in college, but she was nineteen at the time and he was a total fox, so he didn't count.

Maybe Matt really was too busy, or he'd decided she was too much work. It wouldn't be the first time a guy had ended up there, she moped as she started pulling blue painter's tape from around one of the window frames. Whatever the reason, he'd made it clear he wasn't interested.

It was time to let it go and move on.

Caty McKenzie was driving him nuts.

It was past midnight, and even though he was beat, Matt lay awake listening to the breeze rustling through the branches outside the open windows. The first couple of nights, he couldn't sleep because it felt awkward to be in what he still considered his father's room. Finally, he slept because he was too exhausted to care.

During his trip to Charlotte, he'd tried to put her out of his mind, but she'd kept popping up. He'd wanted to call her a dozen times since their last meeting, just to see how she was doing. He couldn't imagine how it would feel to find out your life could have been completely different if someone had just told you the truth.

But every time his finger hovered over her number, he hesitated. Part of him wanted to see her, hear her mock something the same way he would have done. See the twinkle in those dark green eyes while she teased him. He wanted to wrap his arms around her and kiss her, to prove to himself that it was nothing special. That she was just like all the other women he'd dated.

Then he'd think: What if she wasn't? What if he kissed

her and it was amazing, and he did something stupid like tell her how much he loved being with her? She was pretty, but he'd dated models, so that wasn't it. She was funny, but so were other women. That left only one thing and, as much as he hated to admit it, Matt couldn't ignore the obvious.

She was smart. More than intelligent, she had a genuine compassion for people, a way of drawing them out of themselves and making them feel that she understood. She'd done that for him so many times, he couldn't keep track of them all. No one had ever worked that hard with him.

Caty was fun to be with, and she'd proven to be a solid friend when he desperately needed one. She didn't hassle him, but she didn't let him get by with the stonewalling that usually kept people at a respectable distance. Ignoring that, she'd shoved into his comfort zone and forced him to open up. At first, it was just a sliver, but the crack widened a little more every time he saw her.

Somewhere along the line, it had become an alarming gap in his defenses. Who'd have thought he needed to guard himself against a woman who probably weighed a hundred pounds with a pocketful of quarters? The trouble was, the more he tried not to think about her, the more she occupied his thoughts.

Aggravated beyond belief, he pulled a pillow over his face and pictured a blank white wall. When his mind wandered to Caty, he forced it back to staring at that wall.

Finally, he bored himself to sleep.

Caty was up to her elbows in semigloss white paint when her cell phone rang. She'd spent the past couple of days sanding, repairing and painting the detailed trim her grandfather had milled himself. In all that time not one person had called. Consequently, she had no idea where the phone was. From her cramped position in the downstairs hallway, she decided the phone was in her bedroom and she'd never get to it in time to answer the call. She worked another half hour until all the baseboards for the first floor were done.

She went into the kitchen to wash her hands. While she was rinsing, someone started knocking on her front door.

"Just a minute!" Grabbing a paper towel, she dried her hands on her way to the door.

On the other side was Matt, wearing one motorcycle helmet and holding another. "You know your porch light's out?"

So much for giving up on him.

The moment she saw him, her heart leaped into her throat. Crazy as it seemed, he looked taller and even more handsome than she remembered. His motorcycle wasn't bad, either.

To cover her reaction to him, she craned her neck around the doorway and checked the old coach light. "I didn't notice. I'll find my step stool and replace it later."

"It's pretty dark out here. I can do it now if you want."

His easygoing tone couldn't disguise the fact that he was worried about her. It was so sweet, she couldn't help smiling. "You didn't come all the way in here on a weeknight to tell me my porch was dark, did you?"

"Not exactly. I'm headed out to Ryker's Ridge." He offered her that charmingly crooked grin and the spare helmet. "Wanna come?"

Caty was surprised to find that she did. Even if it meant hanging on the back of his Harley for dear life. Or maybe *because* she'd be hanging on the back of his Harley for dear life.

She could try claiming they were just friends out for

a ride, but it would be a lie. Matt wasn't the type to be "just friends" with a woman for long. More important, it wouldn't take much nudging for her to start falling for his rough-around-the-edges bad-boy act. Considering his much broader experience, she had no doubt he'd picked up on that long before she had.

So, very reluctantly, she shook her head. "I can't."

He didn't say anything, but continued to hold the helmet where she could reach it. It was burgundy, with gold speckles and an amber visor. She was dying to slip it on and go wherever he wanted to take her.

Instead, like a parrot, she repeated, "I can't."

He studied her as if she was a new species he'd discovered. She could just imagine it: Woman Immune to Sawyer Charm. Never Before Seen in the Wild.

Still staring at her, he lowered the helmet and rested it against his thigh. "Mind if I ask why?"

She could have told him she had too much to do, but he'd see right through that excuse. It was almost nine, and any sane person would have quit working by now. She could tell him she was afraid of motorcycles, but that would be a lie. They fascinated her, especially the sleek burgundy-and-black machine parked at the end of her walk, chrome glowing in the hazy moonlight. Looking very dangerous, it promised the adventure and excitement she didn't allow herself to want.

Like its owner, she realized with a jolt.

Then again, David had been solid and stable, and he'd broken her heart. Caty felt as though she was spinning in circles, trying to balance past failure with the slim possibility of success with someone who was the polar opposite.

It wasn't the kind of decision a girl should make on the spur of the moment, so she reverted to calm, logical rules. Since he knew how she'd lost her job, she was confident he wouldn't press her to break the rules again. "You're a client, and I make it a policy not to get personal with my clients."

"You don't charge me, so that policy doesn't apply."

"Nice try."

Her heart really wasn't in this argument, but she had to stick to her guns. She knew going with him tonight would lead to more, and she just couldn't let that happen. Hoping to appear determined rather than desperate, she folded her arms and did her best to glare up at him.

"Okay." Leaning back against the porch column, he fixed her with a no-nonsense look. "You're fired."

"That's not funny," she huffed, barely resisting the urge to smack him.

"I'm not kidding."

"You'd fire me so we can go for a ride? That's nuts."

"I can get a lawyer outta the phone book," he reasoned. "You, sweetheart, are one of a kind."

"I really hate that name," she reminded him curtly. "Can't you come up with something else?"

He studied her briefly. "Babe."

"Worse."

"Shortcake."

"Insulting," she shot back.

Now he was grinning, and she realized he was enjoying their battle of wits immensely. "How 'bout punkin?"

She gave him her sternest lawyer's stare, which only made him laugh. He didn't shift from his casual pose, didn't even remotely hint at touching her. But something in his manner changed, making it clear he had every intention of getting closer eventually. Much closer.

"I haven't heard from you since you left here a week ago," she challenged, stalling for time to think. It had actually been eight days, but she didn't want him to think she'd been counting them. "What changed?"

"It was eight days," he corrected her. "And I missed you."

I missed you, too! she wanted to shout, but she held back. The fact that he'd counted the time they were apart made her heart do a little flip. He wouldn't have done that if he didn't really like her. Would he?

The more mature part of her shoved in, reminding her that offering her heart to someone gave him a chance to shred it and toss it back.

After some serious internal battling, she called it a draw. "Why me?"

Heaving a frustrated sigh, he shook his head. "I have no idea. Maybe you can help me figure it out," he added with a wry grin.

It was the grin that did it. To her knowledge, she'd never baffled any man she'd met. It was flattering to discover she had even a smidgen of the feminine mystique she'd read about in all those gushy romance novels.

Before she could analyze the whole thing to death, she said, "I've never been on a motorcycle."

The grin widened, and a rare flicker of mischief lit his eyes. "I can fix that."

"I'm a mess, though. Give me a few minutes?"

"Sure."

"I'd invite you in, but the place is a disaster."

He looked over her head at her disheveled living room. "Looks like daisies in there."

She waited for the punch line, but it never came. "And?"

"It's pretty," he replied with a shrug. "It suits you."

She could feel a blush creeping up her cheeks, and she was glad he couldn't see it. "Thanks. I won't be long."

"No rush. If you bring me a bulb, I'll replace this one."

She had no idea where she'd put the spare lightbulbs, so she unscrewed one from a wall sconce and handed it to him. Then she hurried upstairs and took a quick shower to remove the worst of the paint from her skin. A few stubborn specks clung to her hands and arms, but a quick look in the mirror assured her there weren't any on her face. She looped her wet hair into a ponytail and pulled on jeans and a faded pink Life is good T-shirt.

As she did the clasp on the silver necklace she'd bought that morning, she silently cautioned her excited reflection to at least pretend to be cool. She'd spent a lot of time hemming and hawing over Matt, and she didn't want him picking up on her dilemma. It would only make him unbearable. One minute she thought he was a bad boy with a heart of gold. The next, her pragmatic side reminded her of three very good reasons she couldn't get involved with him.

Client. Wanderer. Faithless.

He'd taken care of the first, and the second she could work around. The third, not so much. She'd made that mistake with David, and she had no intention of repeating it.

The seesaw thing was pretty much pointless, since she'd been trained to debate all angles of any subject. One thing she couldn't deny: when Matt showed up on her porch tonight, she was ridiculously happy to see him. She was either falling for him or she needed to get out more. Maybe both.

Pushing yet another unanswerable question aside, she all but skipped down the stairs and out the front door.

"Much better," she said, approving of the new light. Then she frowned. "I really need to paint these old floorboards."

"Tomorrow," he said, handing her the spare helmet. "Is that a new necklace?"

"Yeah, I bought it today." She held out the silver circle so he could see it.

"'If you can believe, all things are possible.'" He read the inscription out loud. "I've seen that somewhere before."

It's from the Bible, she wanted to say. But she settled for, "It's one of my favorite sayings."

"Pretty."

"Thanks. I left the windows open to vent the house," she said as she climbed onto the back of his bike. "Is it supposed to rain?"

"Nope."

With that, he swiveled her visor closed, effectively telling her to shut up. But she was so jazzed about actually being on a big, bad Harley, she decided to let it go. He grasped the handlebars and kicked the engine into gear. She'd seen enough people on bikes to know she was supposed to wrap her arms around him and lean against his back. Suddenly shy, she hesitated, and he glanced over his shoulder at her.

Reaching down, he patted one of the handles welded to the frame by her seat. It seemed less intimate, so she went with that. Once they were out of town, he sped up and she felt as if she was going to fly right off the bike. Finally she decided it wasn't a hug, it was survival, and she slid her arms around his waist. Now that she was shielded from the wind, she could actually enjoy the sensation of the world rushing past.

Exhilarating and a little terrifying, it was like nothing she'd ever experienced. She loved the open-air feeling of her convertible, but this was a notch beyond that. It actually felt as though they were flying over the road, rather than rolling on top of it.

When they reached the ridge, she got off and popped

her helmet loose. "Okay, now I get the whole motorcycle thing. That was so cool."

Still astride the seat, Matt removed his helmet and grinned at her. "Glad you liked it. Most women don't."

"How many times do I have to tell you?" she retorted while she restrung her disheveled ponytail. "I'm not like most women."

"Good to know." He looked out over the valley with a sigh. "I love this place. My buddies and I used to camp up here. Fish all day, cook whatever we caught over a campfire and just hang. No girls," he added before she could ask.

"Sounds perfect." She found a boulder with a bowl-shaped dip in the top and settled in, admiring the view. "This is really beautiful."

"You've never been up here?" he asked, stretching out on the ground in front of the rock. He seemed to be going out of his way to give her some space, which made her more comfortable. Considering her schoolgirl reaction to what he'd said earlier, keeping her distance from him seemed like the smart thing to do.

"I wasn't allowed. It was make-out central, and my grandparents didn't want me getting into trouble."

Matt chuckled. "Yeah, it was one of John's favorite spots."

They sat quietly for a while, and Caty felt the knots in her sore muscles unravel as the peaceful evening air settled around her. Night birds gliding overhead called out to each other, their voices blending with hundreds of frogs and crickets to echo through the air.

Far removed from the hectic pace she'd kept up for so long, she closed her eyes and just breathed.

"Caty, can I ask you something personal?"

Without opening her eyes, she smiled. "Sure."

"What happened with David?"

She opened her eyes to see him still staring out over the valley. "Nothing, really. We just wanted different things."

"Were you together a long time?"

"Almost four years. We met in law school and then worked at the same firm in Boston. At the time, it seemed like the ideal arrangement."

"What changed?" he asked casually, as if they were talking about the weather. But she'd learned something about him in the past few weeks. The more distant he tried to appear, the harder the subject was for him to talk about.

"David started wanting different things, is all. He liked the money and prestige that came with being an attorney at a big firm. I saw it as a way to get experience so I could open my own practice someday."

"You were smarter than him."

She laughed. "What makes you say that?"

"Most guys can't be with a woman who's smarter than them. Makes 'em feel insecure."

"I never really thought about it," Caty admitted. "Our main argument was over God."

That got Matt's attention, and he spun to face her. Slinging an arm over his bent knee, he said, "Really? Why?"

"I believed, he didn't. There's really not any middle ground."

After a pause, Matt said, "I still do, you know."

Even though she knew perfectly well what he meant, she wanted him to say it. "Do what?"

"Believe in God," he confessed with a scowl. "Sometimes I think it'd be easier if I didn't. You can't get ignored by someone who doesn't exist."

The raw emotion in his voice broke her heart. "What makes you think He ignored you?"

Another pause, warning her they were on painful ground.

"When Mom got sick, Dad told me God would work miracles. You just had to ask. So every morning and every night, I got down on my knees and prayed for her to get better." He swallowed so hard, she could almost feel it. "The day we buried her was the last time I ever set foot in a church. God ignored me, and I returned the favor."

If there was any chance for them to have a future, this was a pivotal moment. Inspiration struck, and Caty asked, "Who chose your name?"

"Mom," he answered with a puzzled look. "Why?"

"Do you know what it means?"

"Nope."

He looked down when he said it. Anybody with ten minutes of psych training would know it meant he was lying, but she decided to let it go.

"It means 'beloved of God.' You were her first child, and she didn't give you that name by mistake." Reaching out, she gently touched his cheek. "She wanted you to feel that always, Matthew."

He uncoiled from his casual position and settled a hand on either side of her, effectively trapping her between his massive arms. The remote interest in his eyes deepened to an intensity that should have frightened her. The fact that it didn't meant something, but she didn't have time to ponder that right now.

"Why do you call me that?" he asked so quietly she almost didn't hear him.

She wasn't afraid of him because he'd proven time and again he'd never hurt her. But she was very much afraid of how deeply she could see into him when he was this close. She had a feeling it scared him, too.

"No one calls me that. Anymore," he added, a child's anguish flooding his eyes.

It was the name his mother had used.

Caty knew it with an aching certainty she'd seldom felt. While she searched for a way to ease the pain she'd caused him, he edged closer. She knew she should move away, but she couldn't make herself do it.

"No one's ever looked at me the way you do," he murmured, looking as bewildered as she felt. "You see something in me."

Stunned by the conviction in his voice, she could only nod.

"What?" His chest pressed into hers, and she felt the insistent beating of his heart. "What do you see?"

"A good heart," she heard herself say. Groaning inwardly, she waited for him to laugh.

He didn't.

"Most folks think I don't have one."

"They're wrong," she said indignantly, angry with the faceless people who'd made him feel like less than he was. "You have an amazing heart. It just takes a little effort to get through."

"Is that what you're after? To get through?"

He hadn't moved, but she could feel the warmth of his skin through his shirt. A current of awareness coursed along every nerve, making her feel as though she'd been spinning in circles and had suddenly stopped.

Somehow she assembled enough sense to shoot back, "I'm not after anything."

"I know." In the near darkness, she saw him smile. "That's what I like most about you."

When his mouth settled over hers, she gladly let the wave of emotions sweep her away. Falling for Matt Sawyer was quite possibly the biggest risk she'd ever take in her life. And she didn't care.

Chapter Ten

Filthy and so tired his bones felt like pudding, Matt dragged himself in from another round of haying. One perk of this farming thing: he was in better shape than when he'd been hitting a gym four days a week. But he was done for the week, and even though he would have happily fallen right into bed, he'd let John talk him into going to the short-track races out at the fairgrounds. Honestly, it wasn't that tough. Matt hadn't been to a race yet, and the season was almost over.

After a quick shower, he dialed Caty's number. They hadn't been together since their ride, and he hadn't talked to her all week. He actually missed hearing her voice. Accustomed to taking care of only himself, he wasn't used to feeling this way. It didn't sit well yet, but when she answered the phone, he felt a lot better.

"I take it this means the hay is in," she said.

"Finally. How are your floors?"

"Done and sealed. The guy on HGTV says I can walk on them Monday."

Even though the words sounded like her, something was off. Maybe it was the phone.

He chuckled. "Congratulations. John and I are going out to the fairgrounds for the races. Wanna come?"

"That's right, it's Saturday. So that's where all the neighbors are."

"You forgot what day it is?" he teased.

"You'd think I'd figure it out when my house is the only one in town with lights on. Thanks for thinking of me, but I'm totally shot. I'm headed upstairs for bed."

Thanks for thinking of me? That was the kind of thing you said when you were blowing someone off. When you'd rather gnaw off your own arm than spend any amount of time with them, but were too nice to come right out and say it.

"Something wrong?" he asked.

"Just tired."

"You've been working way too hard. Come have some fun."

"I think I've had enough fun for a while."

There was a warning note in her voice he didn't like. When it came to people, especially women, he always fared better face-to-face. He could read her expression and figure out what was really going on.

"Why don't I grab some supper and come by? We'll have something to eat and—"

"No," she cut him off sharply. "Do not come over here."

That was pretty clear, but he was still confused. "Okay, I give up. What's going on?"

She let out a sigh that crackled in the phone. "Are you serious?"

Caught off guard by her attitude, he fell back on a classic guy's excuse. "I'm not a mind reader. Spell it out for me."

"I haven't heard from you all week," she shot back,

irritation clear through the static in the line. "I took that to mean you were done with me."

Done? Matt's chest seized up tight, and he rubbed at what he thought was a pulled muscle. It didn't help.

"I've been busy," he explained.

"So have I. That's not the problem, and you know it."

"Then what's the problem?"

Silence.

It stretched on for what felt like forever. When she finally spoke, he heard tears in her voice. Tears he'd caused, even though he'd done everything he knew not to hurt her. "That night at the pond, I thought we connected."

"We did." It killed him to admit it, but it was true. That was the night he'd realized just how special she was. He should have told her, but something always seemed to stop him. Timing. Circumstances. Blind fear.

"Then we started working on things together. My house, Ethan's estate. Even though it was tough sometimes, I thought we had fun."

"We did."

"Things seemed to be going well. Slow but well. I understand being careful, believe me. Then up at the ridge…" Her voice trailed off, then turned on him with a bite. "Whenever we start getting closer, you pull away. Maybe other women are willing to chase after you, but I'm not."

He knew she had a temper—it had even been directed his way more than once. But this was more than anger. It sounded as if she'd given up on him.

Hoping to smooth his way out of trouble, he said, "I know I'm not easy. I'm working on it."

"Matthew, at your age, you should pretty much be done."

With that, she hung up.

Stunned by the nasty turn their conversation had taken,

he eventually hung up, too. For a few minutes he stared at the phone. Expecting to hear her unique country-ballad ring, see her number on the caller ID. Waiting for her to call and tell him she understood and would be patient with him while he sorted things out. But she didn't.

Kicking himself for screwing up yet another good thing, he decided to take his bike out for some fresh air. After leaving a note telling John he'd meet him at the track, Matt took the long route, hoping the winding roads would help clear his mind. Women came and went, he reminded himself as the wind whipped past his helmet. That was how his life worked.

The problem was, it didn't work that way anymore. When had that happened? He still hadn't come up with an answer when he arrived at the fairgrounds. He strolled along the front of the grandstand and found John in the third row from the top, waving like a maniac.

"You're just in time for the second feature." Grinning, his little brother offered up a plate of greasy fries. "Want some?"

The cars fired, and Matt knew his voice wouldn't carry over the sound, so he settled for shaking his head. John shrugged and focused on the action as the green flag dropped. Most dirt-track races were wrecks waiting to happen, so it didn't take long for trouble to strike.

"Oh, man!" John exclaimed as a car hit the retaining wall. "That'll leave a mark."

"No doubt," Matt said absently, pulling his phone out of his jeans pocket to check for messages. Nothing.

"That's like the tenth time you've done that," John chided. "I could've come with Annie Granger, but I put her off to hang out with my big brother."

"Sorry."

"Are you waiting on a call or something?"

"No, but if it rang I wouldn't hear it over the cars."

John gave him a knowing guy's grin. "You should've made her come. Caty loves the races, and she could use a night out for some fun."

"Yeah, well, she said no."

"She's good at that," John agreed, as the man in front of him stood to go down to the concession stand. Taking advantage of the clear space, John stretched his legs out over the seat. "Y'know, she's the only girl who ever turned me down."

"That makes two of us."

John's lazy mood suddenly shifted, and he whipped around to face Matt. "What did you do?"

"Calm down, Goldilocks. It wasn't like that."

His hotheaded little brother cooled a few degrees and sat back. "Then how *was* it?"

"I wrecked things."

"How?"

"How should I know?" he snarled. John looked doubtful, and Matt realized he wasn't being honest. With himself. To avoid John's eyes, he looked down at his phone while he flipped it over and over in his hands. "She said when we started getting closer, I pulled away."

"I've seen you do that before. Like you don't wanna get too attached to people and then lose them. The girls and I do it, too, but you're the worst."

Matt met his brother's sympathetic gaze, and John smiled. "Caty told you not to come over, didn't she?"

"Very clearly."

He chuckled. "She's got a lot of spunk. That's what I like most about her."

Matt finally cracked a smile. "Yeah, me, too."

"Let her cool off, go over tomorrow," John advised, folding himself back into his spot so the guy in front of him could sit back down. "She's stubborn, but she's got a real soft heart. Give her a chance to remember what she likes about you, then talk to her. It'll go better that way."

Matt suddenly had a newfound respect for John's take on women, Caty in particular. "When did you get to be so smart?"

"Learned most of it from you," he replied with a broad grin. "Except for the arguing part. I'm no good at that."

The whole time they'd been discussing Caty, Matt had a vague prickly feeling under his skin. Thinking it was from his peeling sunburn, he scratched it, but it wouldn't go away. He sat through another feature, thinking it would pass if he distracted himself. It didn't.

When his thoughts drifted to Caty, the weird sensation intensified. It was probably nothing, just that he felt bad about upsetting her. Forgoing John's advice, he decided to stop by on the way home and see if she might still be up. She'd been on her way to bed a couple of hours ago, but maybe she'd changed her mind.

So he made up an excuse about being tired, which he was, and getting out ahead of the crowd. Shaking his head, John grinned and wished him a good night.

Something was wrong.

Matt didn't know what, exactly, but his instincts were all on alert as he hurried out to his bike. The roads were empty, so he pushed the Harley far past seventy and made it into Harland in record time. Main Street was quiet, its single traffic light blinking amber this time of night. On one of the side streets, something else was flickering a more ominous color.

When Matt turned onto Oak Street, his heart shot into his throat. Flames were pouring through the open lower windows of Caty's house, and inside he could see them licking the ceiling.

Forcing himself to think, he shut off the bike and let it fall while he pulled out his phone and dialed 911. "House fire at 14 Oak Street in Harland. Hurry."

The operator was still talking when he dropped the phone and ran toward the back of the house. An old oak was silhouetted in the eerie flickers, offering him a way up. Some of the branches creaked under his weight as he scrambled up, but they held. Standing on the back porch roof, he pounded on the closed window.

"Caty!"

He waited a few seconds, then pounded again. Nothing. He tried the window, but it was either locked or painted shut. Glancing around, he looked for another way in. There wasn't one.

Most of the volunteer fire department was at the fairgrounds, and it would take them a while to get here. Matt peeled off the flannel he was wearing over his T-shirt and wrapped it around his hand. One shot put him through the old window and the jagged glass raked his arm in retaliation. Ignoring it, he reached in to unlock and raise the window before climbing through.

He couldn't see a thing.

Smoke immediately clogged his throat, and he tied the shirt around his face. Something wet hit his cheek, and he vaguely realized it must be blood. Pushing the thought aside, he felt his way along the wall. Bathroom. Spare room. He pivoted and carefully avoided the head of the stairs as he crossed the hall.

Without sight, it was tough going, but he found the open door to Caty's room and felt his way over to her bed. Squinting to keep some of the smoke out of his eyes, he tried to shake her awake. When that didn't work, he put a hand on her back to feel her breathing.

Nothing.

Panic swelled in his chest, and with effort he swallowed it back. Light as she was, he lifted her easily and put her over his shoulder in the fireman's carry he'd seen in movies. Then he crept through the hallway, searching for the window. A pale shaft of moonlight penetrated the smoke, and he corrected his course to head in the right direction.

How he got down the tree without dropping Caty, he'd never know. But when he came around the side of the house, the Harland engine was just pulling up, with an ambulance close behind. He knew enough to stay out of the way, so he dragged himself to the Fairmans' side porch steps and sank down in relief.

While his lungs coughed out the worst air they'd ever taken in, he rested Caty's head on his shoulder so the fresher air could revive her.

"Come on, shortcake," he begged, hoping the nickname would get a rise out of her. "You're okay now."

But she wasn't. She was pale and unconscious, and he still wasn't sure if she was breathing. Shaking with fear, he gave her up to the EMTs, waving them off him so they could focus on her.

They strapped an oxygen mask on her and whisked her into the ambulance, which took off at the kind of speed that told him this was a true emergency. Leaning back, Matt watched them go as the second floor of Caty's house fell into the living room. Still struggling to breathe normally, he tilted his head back and stared up at the clouds of smoke billowing into the black sky.

And then, from nowhere, he heard his own voice.

"I don't know if You're still listening to me, but don't You dare—"

No. You didn't threaten God.

With a sigh, Matt swiveled off the porch and hit his

knees. The humble pose made him feel vulnerable, but he did it anyway. This was for Caty, and he wanted to do it right. Resting his elbows on the top step, he ignored the tears rolling down his cheeks. Silencing the protest clanging in his head, he let his heart decide what to say.

"Please don't let her die."

"Matt!"

He looked back to find John racing toward him. John skidded to a stop beside him, landing on his knees with an arm around Matt's shoulders.

"Are you okay?"

"More or less. They took Caty to the hospital."

Without hesitation, John tipped his head down, and for once Matt envied the way his brother could open himself up so readily. Maybe it did make life easier, the way Marianne insisted.

"Come on," John prompted as he stood. "I'll drive."

It was a total reversal of their usual roles, John taking care of him. Out of habit, Matt almost refused. Then he realized it meant a lot to John to take over this way. "Okay. Thanks."

When they turned to go, Matt saw the glint of something in the grass. Leaning down, he fished out Caty's silver necklace. In the swirling glare of emergency lights, he read the inscription.

If you can believe, all things are possible.

Now he remembered where he'd read that before. Ethan's devotional book had been open to that verse the day he died. It was easy to think that, like Caty, this was one of his father's favorite sayings. It summed them both up perfectly. Always believing, never giving up, even when it might be the most sensible thing to do.

Crazy as it seemed, in his heart Matt knew his instinct

to check on Caty had been no accident. God had known she was in danger, and He sent Matt to save her.

As he folded the necklace into his fist, he knew this was the answer to his desperate prayer. Despite everything he'd done wrong, all the mistakes he'd made, God was still listening.

Where was she?

Caty tried to move, then blearily realized her feet weren't on the ground. A thick fog enveloped her brain, making it hard to think. She fought her way through it, like a diver reaching for the surface. When she finally broke free, she cautiously opened her eyes, wondering what she might see.

"Hey, there." Leaning forward from a small chair, Matt smiled. "Feeling better?"

Was she sick? Caty wondered. When she tried to ask, she realized there was something covering her face. She reached up to move it, but he stopped her with a gentle hand.

"Leave it be, Caty. You need it."

"Why?" she asked, her voice muffled by a plastic mask.

He didn't want to tell her. She could see it in his eyes. Now that her brain was starting to function more normally, she noticed the creases of black on his face, more traces of it on his clothes. Trying not to panic, she repeated her question more insistently.

"There was a fire," he said finally. "But you're gonna be fine."

As he pulled the light blanket up for her, she saw the raw cuts on his hands and forearms. Ignoring his protest, she pulled the oxygen mask aside. "You got me out, didn't you?"

He cracked a pale version of his wry grin. "Well, I was in the neighborhood, so I thought I'd stop by."

"And rescue me from a burning house," she finished. "Even though I explicitly told you not to come over."

"I'm not good at taking orders."

"Thank God for that."

"I'm with you on that one," he quickly agreed.

From him, the comment came as a complete shock. She shook her head in amazement, which made her dizzy. She stopped, but it took a few seconds for the world to quit spinning. "What happened?"

"No clue. When I got there, the whole first floor was gone. I went up that tree in back to the window at the head of the stairs."

"But it was painted shut."

"Not anymore."

Ignoring the IV line in her arm, she reached for his battered hand. It took more strength than it should have, but she caught it between both of hers for a grateful squeeze. "Thank you."

It was as though a breeze came through and blew the gray clouds from his eyes, leaving behind the vivid blue she'd come to adore. "You're welcome."

After a few relatively normal breaths, she asked, "What made you think to stop by?"

He shrugged. "Just wanted to make sure you were okay."

There was something he wasn't telling her. She knew it by the way his gaze had dropped to their intertwined hands. Ordinarily she'd press for details, but she didn't have the heart to harass him when he'd risked his life to save her.

Instead she asked, "How bad is it?"

"I'm not an expert or anything."

"How bad?"

He hesitated, then lifted his head to meet her eyes. "John and I left just after the second floor caved in."

The news hit her like a physical blow, and she was grateful for the pillows holding her up. She absorbed it as well as she could, fighting off tears, which would only make her choke and cause some kind of medical alert she wanted to avoid. Right now she wasn't up to sharing her room with anyone but Matt.

"I found this out front," he said, holding up her necklace. Reaching around her neck, he fastened it for her. "The nurse said you could have it back once you woke up."

She tried to thank him, but she didn't have the strength to form the words. Someone knocked on the door, and she recognized the Harland fire chief.

"I'll handle him," Matt offered.

"Leave the door open."

"Sweetheart—"

"Leave the door open," she repeated, "or I'll talk to him myself. And don't call me that."

He muttered something unspeakable, then said more loudly, "Stubborn isn't the word for you, y'know that?"

"Lucky for you," she reminded him as she sank back into her pillows. "Anybody else would've given up on you the first time we met."

He gave her something between a scowl and a smile. "Put that oxygen back on."

The room was starting to spin again, and she gladly complied. Matt left her room but held the door ajar with his boot.

"How's she doing, Matt?"

"Okay, more or less. They're keeping her overnight just to be safe."

"Good idea."

"How're things at Caty's place?" Matt asked. "Are all your guys okay?"

"A few cuts and bruises, but mostly they're fine. The house is another story. We're still not sure what happened, but it smells like a chemical plant in there."

"She's been redoing the floors," Matt explained. "The sealer was still wet."

"That explains it. Old house like that, it was probably electrical. It wouldn't take much to ignite those solvents, and with the sealer all over it would've spread fast. The carport fell in, but we managed to move her car, so that's something."

"How'd you move it without the keys?"

"Same way you would, son."

They both laughed, and their conversation switched over to the chief's beloved '57 Chevy. Once they started talking cylinders and pistons, Caty lost interest.

Ironically, she'd bought smoke detectors to replace the old ones but hadn't gotten around to installing them. They were probably lumps of melted plastic on the kitchen counter, sealed in their boxes. Assuming she still had a kitchen counter.

Despite her best efforts to hold them back, tears spilled over and down her cheeks. She wasn't into material things, but anything she did value was in her house. She could buy a new phone and computer, and her important files were locked inside the heavy, fireproof cabinet. The pictures and antiques, wrapped up in memories of the only home she remembered, were irreplaceable.

Over the years, she'd lost the people she loved most one by one. Now the house that embodied her entire history was gone. Even in her state, she knew it was irrational, but she couldn't help feeling as though another member of her family had died, leaving her to figure out a way to keep going. Feeling abandoned and lost, she wept because she simply couldn't stop.

Once more the little girl uprooted by tragedy, she felt completely and utterly alone.

Chapter Eleven

Caty slowly opened her eyes, wondering where on earth she was. She lay in the middle of an enormous bed, the covers twisted around her as if she'd been fighting with someone all night long. She closed her eyes, and images faded in and out of her groggy mind like the scene montage at the end of a movie. Endless feet of stained boards, hazy sirens and red lights, the heart-wrenching reality of the fire.

She turned her head away from the horrific memory and into the pillow. It smelled like fresh hay and soap, and she pulled it closer, burying her nose in the comforting smell. Now she remembered.

Last night they had released her from the hospital. Matt had brought her back to the farm and settled her in his own bed. He had sat with her until she fell asleep, and had probably checked on her several times, even though he needed some rest himself. No doubt he'd fielded a hundred anxious questions from his family so she wouldn't have to face them.

That meant it was Monday. According to the rehab expert on HGTV, she would have been able to walk on her floors today. But it hadn't worked out that way. She was in someone else's house, wearing someone else's clothes. Figuring she had a right to wallow, she started a mental list of everything she'd lost.

Before long, she was so depressed that she went back to sleep just to make it stop.

Matt had never been so tired in his life.

It was more than fatigue, and his back protested as he reached down to slide his mud-caked boots onto the back porch. He was used to working hard, but it had been balanced with a lot of playtime. In his off hours, he would unwind with his bike, running friends' ATVs, playing shortstop for a fairly competitive softball team.

Now it seemed that all he did was work. When he had come back for the funeral, the harvest had been behind by several days. Somehow they'd trimmed it to only a couple. If the weather held, by the end of the week they'd actually be on top of things. If that happened, he promised himself, he'd sleep all weekend. *The thrilling life of a farmer,* he groused as he let the door slam behind him.

Kyle was doing his homework at the kitchen table, while Marianne corrected papers from her own class. Pointing to something in his book, she focused on Kyle while she explained it. He responded, and she smiled, nodding while he wrote the answer on the line.

The cozy scene reminded Matt of a Norman Rockwell drawing, the kind that could soften even the hardest heart. To his surprise, the nasty thoughts whirling through his head vanished, replaced by something he could only describe as pride.

This was his family.

Despite what they'd gone through, they were doing well. He couldn't quite believe it, but he was glad he'd decided to stay. Not wanting to interrupt the lesson, he grabbed some clean clothes from the basket on the counter and went into the bathroom for a quick shower. When he came out, Kyle looked up.

"Hey, Uncle Matt. How was your day?"

"Fine. How 'bout yours?"

"Not so good." The poor kid looked absolutely miserable. "I failed my math test."

Standing, Marianne began to pull dishes from the cupboards. "There's a makeup tomorrow. He just needs a little tutoring."

Matt looked over Kyle's shoulder to see what he was working on. "Looks familiar. Maybe I can help."

After he'd blurted that out, Matt wondered if he'd overstepped his bounds. Marianne was pretty fussy about the kids, and she might not appreciate his interfering.

"That would be great, Matt. Thanks." The dryer buzzed on the side porch, and she gave him a smile before heading out to pull the laundry.

It had been a while since he'd done third-grade math, but he was one up on Kyle, so they worked through it together. Matt wasn't known for his teaching skills, but helping his eager nephew required less patience than he'd anticipated. When the approach clicked, Kyle's bright grin was all the reward he needed.

"I think I get it," Kyle said, eyes wide with excitement. "Can we do a couple more to make sure?"

Matt jotted down six fresh problems, and Kyle got them all right.

"Good job," Matt congratulated him, patting his shoulder. "You'll ace that makeup test."

"Thanks, Uncle Matt."

After a quick hug, Kyle ran outside to his bike, picking up Tucker along the way. With a lot of whooping and barking, they raced past John's house and over the crest of the hill.

"They'd better be back in time for supper," Marianne commented as she returned to the kitchen.

When she started spooning some of her homemade chicken soup into a bowl, Matt asked, "What are you doing?"

"Taking this up to Caty. She's still not feeling well."

"She was fine when I saw her this morning."

Marianne set the ladle down and gave him her I'm-worried look. "It's been four days since the fire. I don't think it's physical anymore."

"Treating her like an invalid won't help any." His exhausted muscles protesting, he pushed off from the table and stood. "I'm gonna go talk to her."

"Matt, that house meant everything to her, and it'll take her a while to get past what happened. You have to be patient."

"If that was me up there—" he pointed at the ceiling "—what would you do?"

Her lips crinkled in a smirk that made him think of the smart-aleck little girl she used to be. "Rent a crane and haul you out of bed."

"Why would you treat her any different?"

"Because she's Caty."

"Not right now, she's not," he argued on his way out. "But she will be."

"Be nice!"

Furious with himself for not acting sooner, he ignored her warning. Caty was like a bright red rose, not a shrinking violet. Because he had a soft spot for her, he'd allowed her to drift along, rather than encouraging her to stand on her own two feet and pick up her life where she'd left off.

The brooding was over, he vowed as he knocked on his bedroom door.

She didn't answer. Thinking she might be asleep, he eased the door open and peeked inside.

What he saw just about stopped his heart.

She sat on the wide windowsill, staring out at the fields, tears streaming down her face. *Grief-stricken* was the word that came to mind. She'd been through so much, managing Ethan's death, losing her job and now her home. His instinct was to wrap his arms around her and never let anything hurt her again.

But that wouldn't help her regain her confidence. It wouldn't bring back the sweet, understanding woman who'd guided him through the worst time in his life. She needed his help, not his pity.

Steeling himself against her tears, he said, "Supper's ready."

"Thanks. I'm not hungry."

When she dropped her forehead on her bent knees, he almost caved. Reminding himself that she needed strength, not coddling, he strode across the room and stood beside her.

"Caty, look at me."

The sight of her tear-streaked face nearly did him in. He kept to his general plan but changed tactics. Sitting in a chair so they were eye to eye, he waited for her to stop crying. It took longer than he liked, but he knew she wouldn't keep it up for long. She was too proud for that.

Reaching out, he brushed away the last of her tears. "You need to come downstairs and have supper with the family. It'll do us all good."

Her chin trembled, but she didn't start crying again. "I can't."

"You survived all those winters in Boston, didn't you?"

That got him a flicker of a smile. "Yeah."

"Then I think you can manage to come have a meal with us." Standing, he offered his hand. "After that, if you wanna come back up here and blubber, you're welcome to it."

She looked at his hand, then up at him. Temper flared in her eyes, a good sign. In his mind, anger was better than feeling nothing at all.

"You're mean," she announced, swinging down from the windowsill.

She batted his hand away and strolled past him with her cute little nose in the air. Grinning, he followed her downstairs to enjoy the evening with his family.

After Marianne and the kids left for the day, Caty wandered aimlessly through the house. She did little jobs here and there, loading the dishwasher, popping a load of towels into the washing machine, things like that. But Marianne was a ruthlessly efficient housekeeper, and there really wasn't much to do.

Caty was used to long, full days, not hours of nothing to do. She clicked on the TV, but after a half hour of daytime fare she felt her brain starting to get mushy. Marianne had taken her laptop to school, so she couldn't get online. Ethan's collection of books was large, but it was all outdated nonfiction about things she wasn't even remotely interested in.

By nine she was so bored, she actually considered going down to John's to see if anything needed doing there. Then she thought better of it. She adored him, but he was a slob. She was restless, not insane.

Maybe some fresh air would help. When the screen door hinges squeaked, Tucker appeared like a bolt from down the lane, tail and tongue wagging hopefully.

"Morning, boy," she greeted him. "How 'bout a walk?"

Tucker's version of a leisurely stroll was for Caty to mosey along while he ran ahead and looped back to make sure she was still there. He seemed to enjoy it, though, and she admired the cleared fields being plowed under for the winter.

Matt was keeping his word. He didn't like farming, but it looked as though he was making it work. Unfortunately, once the Sawyers' crisis was over, there would be no reason for him to stay in Harland. His heroic rescue of her had driven away the last of her reservations about him, and she couldn't help wondering what his plans were. Now that she no longer had a place to live, she could go anywhere. If he left, he might ask her to go with him. If he did, what would she say?

Caty was used to making decisions for herself. She didn't consider anyone else's opinion, because she didn't have to. But Matt had become so important to her, she couldn't imagine being away from him for long. He totally got her, the way her mind worked, what she truly valued. Their last remaining stumbling block was faith, and since their heart-to-heart out at the ridge, she suspected he was coming around on that one.

While she'd been pondering all that, she'd made a full circuit and found herself back at the house. Her MG was tucked into the barn, waiting for the new keys Matt had ordered from some foreign locksmith. She was dying to take it out for a run, but she didn't know the first thing about hot-wiring a car. With her luck, she'd blow up the engine trying to start it.

A metallic glint caught her eye, and she looked toward it. Matt's truck was parked in the turnaround, the meticulously polished chrome gleaming in the sunshine. A bold idea jumped into her head. Before she could talk herself out of it, Caty ran inside and snatched the truck's spare key from the rack by the door.

She was going to see her house. Matt had told her the second floor had caved in, but maybe it wasn't beyond hope. Some things might have been protected from the fire, and she could salvage some of Gram's treasures. She should also visit the Fairmans, assure them she was all right. They undoubtedly knew where she was, but they were probably worried all the same.

Even with the running boards, Caty had to stretch to climb into the driver's seat. Glancing around, she didn't see anyone, so she quietly closed the door. Then she put the key in and turned it.

The loudest alarm she'd ever heard started shrieking. She tried to remove the key, but it wouldn't budge. To make matters worse, nothing happened when she turned it to start the truck. Feeling stupid, she reached out to open the door.

It was locked.

She tried to unlock it, but the button didn't work. That meant she was stuck until the system eventually disarmed itself. Fortunately, the radio still worked, so she had something to listen to while she waited. Resting her head back against the seat, she turned the volume up so she could hear it over the alarm and passed the time by singing along.

Through the windshield, she saw Matt saunter over the top of a small hill. His amused expression only added insult to injury, and she glared back at him. He stopped just short of the truck and dangled his electronic fob for her to see. He didn't stop the noise, but his meaning was clear enough.

Do you want out?

Folding her arms, she stared out the driver's window at the house. She couldn't hear a thing over the alarm and the music, but she knew he was laughing while he strolled over to the driver's door. She didn't know how he could stand all that racket, but he stood there with his thumb over the disarm button, head cocked with a questioning look.

After another minute, it was too much for her to take. Grinding her teeth, she mouthed *please.*

The alarm stopped abruptly, and too late she remembered how loud the stereo was. She jabbed the off button and was startled by the sudden absence of noise. Her ears would be ringing for a week, she groused, as she keyed the window down to take her medicine.

Matt rested his dusty forearms on the open frame and grinned in at her. "Whatcha doin'?"

"Going into town."

"For?"

"Errands."

Chuckling, he shook his head. "Not really good at this deception thing, are you?"

"Fine," she relented with a frustrated sigh. "I'm going to see my house."

"No." Suddenly, he was deadly serious. Leaning in, he pinned her with one of those don't-mess-with-me looks he still thought would intimidate her. "You're not going there."

"I want to see my house. Maybe there's something I can do."

"Trust me. There's not."

"How do you know?" she reasoned. "You said yourself you're not an expert."

"Honey, it's real bad. I'm not sure it's something you need to see."

She let the annoying nickname go because she could sense him giving in just a little. Following her lawyer's training, she pressed the advantage. "Whether I see it or not, it's still in the same shape. Imagining is much worse than knowing the truth."

Muttering under his breath, he gave her a look that would have been terrifying if his eyes hadn't been twinkling that warm blue. "Why do I get the feeling I'm wasting my breath?"

"It's not my fault you don't know how to argue." Inspiration struck, and she said, "But I wouldn't mind some company."

"A compromise, counselor?" he teased. "I didn't think lawyers knew the concept."

"This one does."

"Good to know." After dusting himself off, he opened the driver's door. When she didn't move, he scowled at her. "My truck."

Deciding they'd wrangled enough for one morning, she slid over to the passenger's seat. "That reminds me, when are my new car keys supposed to get here?"

"Anytime now, I'd think," he answered as he started the engine. As he pulled out of the driveway, he sent her a sideways grin. "See? No sirens."

"I can't believe you armed that thing here in Harland."

"I didn't. I forgot to turn it off. Didn't even think about it till I heard it clanging away. If we were in Charlotte, you'd be in jail."

"I was just borrowing it," she argued halfheartedly.

"Without permission. Correct me if I'm wrong, but I think that makes it stealing."

"I know, and I'm sorry." With an exasperated sigh, she flung her head back onto the headrest. "I'm just so bored! Even though she's so busy, Marianne won't leave me any chores to do. My computer's toast, and I don't have a house to work on. The insurance company is sending me a check, but it won't be enough to build a new house in this century.

I still have some savings, but my student-loan payments are eating that up. Maybe I should use the insurance money to pay them off, but I'd still need a place to live. I just don't know."

The helplessness that had crept into her voice disgusted her. She wasn't the kind of girl who laid out her problems for someone else to fix. She handled things herself, in her own way. The trouble was, she had no idea what to do.

"Don't worry about it. We'll figure something out."

His confidence eased some of her anxiety, and she swiveled her head to look over at him. He had the same dark good looks she remembered from high school, but there was so much more. Formidable as his appearance was, his greatest strength came from inside. And in that moment, she knew.

She was in love with him.

The last man on earth she'd have considered being serious about, and she was completely lost. Everything he'd done the past few weeks told her he felt the same way. He just hadn't said the words. It was hard to be the first one, she knew. You might not hear them back. Worse, you might get that pained look from someone who liked hanging out with you but wasn't ready to pick out china patterns.

Glancing over, he gave her a smile she'd never seen before. Somehow gentle and powerful at the same time, it burrowed into her heart and warmed her from head to toe. He took her hand and kissed it as he looked forward again. "Everything's gonna be fine, sweetheart."

"I really wish you'd think of something else to call me."

"I'll work on it," he promised with a chuckle.

Chapter Twelve

Standing in front of the house she grew up in, Caty waited for reality to settle in. Now she understood why Matt had been so vague about the damage. The charming white cottage was completely gone, replaced by a pile of blackened timber. What was left of the roof rested on top of the debris, as if it was still trying to do its job, even though there was nothing left to protect.

"*Disaster* doesn't really cover it, does it?" she joked to hide her dismay. Matt had climbed into all that to save her, and she felt humbled by the risk he'd taken. Out of respect for him, she swallowed her tears and got practical. "My files were in Grandpa's workroom. Would you mind helping me get the cabinet out?"

"No problem. Why don't you go see Mrs. Fairman?"

"Okay."

"I've got some errands to run. I'll meet you over at Ruthy's."

"Okay," she said again, even though she didn't feel it.

Matt must have heard it in her voice, because he put a strong, comforting arm around her shoulders. "It'll get better."

She looked up at him, and he sealed his promise with

a you-can-count-on-me smile. It did make things feel less dire, and she gave herself up to the luxury of having someone so willing to shield her. Pecking her on the cheek, he turned her away from the ruin of her house and gave her a gentle shove toward the Fairmans'.

Caty walked over and knocked on her neighbor's front door. Beaming, Mrs. Fairman hurried down the hallway and whisked her inside.

"Come in, you poor dear. Would you like some tea?"

"That would be great, thank you."

"George and I have been praying for you every morning," the kind woman told her as she poured water from her whistling teakettle into two dainty floral cups. "We're so sorry about what happened."

"I'm fine, really. Was there any damage here?"

"A few singed azaleas here and there. Nothing to worry about."

After adding a plate of her homemade lemon squares to a tray, she set it on the table. To move the conversation away from the fire, Caty petted Annabelle and asked what she'd missed the past few days. She polished off four lemon squares and drained her tea while Mrs. Fairman caught her up on the news.

The harmless gossip made things feel more normal, and Caty appreciated the distraction. Then Mrs. Fairman got her attention with something else.

"I'm not sure it's my place to say anything," she began with a hesitant look.

Feeling generous, Caty smiled. "Go ahead."

"Your grandmother, God rest her, was a good friend of mine, and we saw most things the same way. I think if she was here, she'd be talking to you about Matt Sawyer."

Caty had no doubt she was right. "Okay."

"He's just bad news, that one. I adored his parents, and

the rest of the family is wonderful. Even the Sawyers have their black sheep, I suppose."

"I suppose," Caty echoed, trying not to smile.

"You're staying out at the farm with him, aren't you?"

"Marianne offered me a place to stay while I sort things out," Caty explained patiently. "There's nothing improper going on, I promise."

"Oh, you don't have to tell me," her hostess assured her, waving away the very idea. "Others around town are talking more than they should about things that don't concern them. I just didn't want you hearing it that way."

Message received. "I appreciate your concern."

"Anyway, in high school, my Deanna—do you remember her, dear?"

Caty recalled a Barbie-ish cheerleader who worked her way through the Wildcats football team every season. Twice. "Yes, ma'am. She was pretty and popular, all rolled into one."

"That's a good description. Such a sweet thing." Her proud smile drooped into a frown of disapproval. "Anyway, she fell hard for Matt Sawyer, and the minute she told him so, he dropped her like it was nothing. Just broke her heart."

Caty was certain there was more to it than that, and she felt obliged to defend him. "That was a long time ago."

The woman leaned in with a knowing look. "Take a little bit of wisdom from an old lady. Men never change. They don't know how."

Caty *hmm*ed at that and tactfully changed the subject. There was no way she'd get into an argument with her thoughtful neighbor over Matt. She'd go after anyone who said a bad word about him. One thing resonated, though, and she resolved to do something about it.

She needed somewhere else to live. Matt didn't care

what people thought any more than she did, but the Sawyers had been through enough the past couple of months.
They didn't deserve to be grist for the town gossip mill.
And if Caty intended to start her own law practice, she
couldn't have people doubting her integrity. Besides being
a personal insult, it would be bad for business.

After twenty minutes, Caty managed to politely extri-
cate herself from the Fairmans' parlor. She didn't know
how long Matt's errands would take, but she hadn't seen
Ruthy in a while, so she headed straight there. No matter
what the problem was, Ruthy was always full of good
ideas. Caty could use some of those about now.

"Hey, you!" Lisa came out from behind the counter to
give her a hug. "It's good to see you out and about."

"It's good to *be* out and about. Is Ruthy here?"

Lisa laughed. "Always. She's in the kitchen experiment-
ing. Go on back."

"Thanks."

Caty poked her head around the doorway to make sure
it was safe. You never knew what might be cooking when
Ruthy was feeling creative. Her chin had a swipe of flour
on it, and she was pensively stirring something in a sauce-
pan, but otherwise things were quiet.

"Knock, knock."

The woman's face lit up, and she dropped her spoon to
give Caty a warm hug. Then she held her away for a thorough looking-over. "How are you?"

"Fine."

Ruthy tipped her head with a chiding look. "That won't
work on me, Caty Lee." She pulled a couple of stools from
under the counter, taking one for herself and patting the
other one. "How are you really?"

Caty took the seat, because there was no refusing her.
"I really am fine. The doctor said my lungs are clear, and

Marianne keeps making all my favorite foods. So, except for the wreck of a house I now own, things are good."

That got her one of those long, penetrating Ruthy looks. Raising a knowing brow, she prompted, "And?"

There was only one thing that could put that sparkle in her eyes, and Caty laughed. "How did you know?"

"It's all over town, sweet pea. Matt's been running wild for so long, it was bound to make news when someone finally tamed him."

"I haven't tamed him. I like him the way he is."

"Praise the Lord!" Ruthy exclaimed. "There's a lot of good in that man. I'm glad he finally found someone who can appreciate him."

"I definitely do," Caty confided. "Maybe more than I should."

"No such thing. If you just give him a chance, he won't let you down."

"Speaking of dependable people, I could use some advice."

"From me?" She looked genuinely surprised. "Whatever for?"

Taking full advantage of the opportunity, Caty spilled her guts. Everything that had plagued her since returning home came tumbling out. Ruthy nodded wisely, offering encouragement at some points, silence at others. Then, since she was on a roll, Caty went for the gold ring.

"Did you know my father?"

Ruthy pressed her lips into a firm line, sorrow filling her normally cheerful blue eyes. "What happened?"

While Caty told her about the letter and photo destroyed in the fire, her eyes welled with tears. "I memorized the whole thing, but it's gone. I was hoping since you and Gram were friends she might have told you something about him."

"The only things she ever said were hateful. I wouldn't repeat them to his child."

"Why did she and Mom hate him so much?"

Ruthy didn't respond immediately. Obviously sifting through memories, she took Caty's hands and gave her a fond smile. "He loved your mother, and now you know he loved you. Isn't that enough?"

"No, it isn't." Caty grasped those flour-covered hands, begging. "I need to know. Please tell me the truth."

"He was married."

All the wonderful images she had of him vaporized. "What?"

"Your mother didn't know at first," Ruthy continued as if it made a difference. "When she found out, she left him."

"But it was too late."

"Don't you dare say it like that," Ruthy snapped, squeezing her hands more tightly. "You're a blessing straight from God, no matter how you came to be. People are much more than their circumstances."

One of the waitresses came to the pass-through to ask Ruthy a question. While she was gone, Caty mulled over what she now knew. She was as illegitimate as a person could get. Not only had her parents not been married to each other, their relationship was a sin. On the sliding scale of right and wrong, that was atrocious. Brian Jameson had not only betrayed his wife, he'd lied to a woman who'd trusted him.

That explained the covert letter, why he'd never tried to find Caty. He had his own family, and she didn't fit into the picture. She should just forget what she'd learned about him and get on with her life.

When Ruthy returned, she had a glass of lemonade for Caty. After a sip, Caty forced a smile. "That must have been tough for you. Thanks."

"You deserve the truth. I only wish I'd thought to tell you sooner."

"You didn't break a promise to Gram or anything, did you?"

"Not really."

Apparently there was more to the story but Ruthy wasn't keen on telling it. Caty wasn't sure she wanted to hear it anyway, so she decided to let it go. "I should let you get back to your cooking," she said, sliding off her stool.

"I've got time before the lunch crowd."

Caty laughed to ease the sting of her next question. "Any advice for a homeless, unemployed attorney?"

The woman gave her a motherly smile and took her hand. "Follow me."

They went up the narrow back stairs to an unlocked door on the second floor. It opened into a small but spotless room, with just enough space for a bed, dresser and kitchenette. A looped-back curtain framed the door of a tiny bathroom.

Ruth Benton was famous for taking in strays, both animal and human. If her character radar approved, she'd offer one of her spare rooms to someone needing a place to stay while they got back on track. Many of them ended up working in her kitchen, at the church or for one of her sons.

On the wall, displayed so it could be seen from every corner of the small apartment, was a sign in a thick black frame.

No Smoking. No Drinking. No Overnight Guests. Beneath the very large letters was a picture of Ruthy wielding a lethal-looking cast-iron frying pan. Her threatening expression said she meant business, but it couldn't mask the sparkle in her eyes. Caty had no doubt that, given the chance, Ruthy could convince the devil himself to rethink his evil ways.

"It's not much," she commented as she opened the windows, "but it's free. The girl who was using it got her own place a couple days ago. It's yours if you want it."

The little studio was well-kept but bland, with cream-colored walls and scarred plank floors. Some new curtains and bedding would spruce things up nicely. "I'm not destitute or anything. I can pay you rent."

"This place comes free of charge," Ruthy informed her sternly. "God's been good to me, and He expects me to pass that along." Her expression softened into a fond smile. "Besides, it'll be nice having you around again. You were always one of my favorite kids."

Being called a kid again made Caty smile. "And you were always one of my favorite grown-ups. If it weren't for you, I wouldn't have gotten my waitressing job in Boston. They said I was trained by the best."

"You were a quick study. I have to get back downstairs, but you're welcome to stay. The key's in the cookie jar."

Thrilled with this sudden good turn, Caty embraced her. "Thanks, Ruthy. You're the best."

"Only to folks who deserve it."

Caty followed her back downstairs and into the dining room. There was some kind of excitement over by the counter, and Ruthy muttered, "Oh, no."

"What?"

"I'm not sure, but Connie's not in her uniform and she's late for work."

"She looks happy, though. It must be a good reason."

Detaching herself from her admirers, Connie floated over and waved a sparkling diamond in their faces. "Jason proposed! We're on our way to Vegas to get married."

Ruthy congratulated her, then said, "I hate to rain on your parade, but did you forget you're working today?"

Connie's delight vanished, and her face twisted with sincere dismay. "I did. Ruthy, I'm sorry. Jason surprised me, and I was so excited I completely forgot. I'll tell him to change our tickets."

"Don't do that," Caty jumped in. "I'll cover for you."

Ruthy turned to her with an astonished look. "Are you sure?"

"I need a job, you need a waitress. Sounds perfect to me."

"Oh, Caty, thank you!" Connie crushed her in an exuberant hug and added one for her boss.

"All right, then." Ruthy opened the antique cash register and handed Connie several twenties. "That's my wedding gift, so you and Jason have fun with it. When you get back, let me know so I can add you back into the schedule."

"I will," she promised, waving on her way out the door.

After Connie had blown out of the diner, Ruthy turned to Caty with a smile. "Do you still remember how to take down an order?"

Matt returned to Harland feeling pretty good about himself. On the passenger seat was the result of his "errands": a big box wrapped in pink confetti paper and topped with a bow that looked like fireworks. Inside was a classy, burgundy-leather case with the newest version of the laptop Caty had lost in the fire. It had meant making a trip into Kenwood, but he didn't mind. He couldn't wait to give it to her.

He'd never let himself get into this situation before, and it should have sent him into a panic. Just the thought of someone depending on him scared him to death. Even worse was the idea of his relying on anyone besides himself. He'd always thought that strength came from standing on your own and taking what came.

Somewhere along the line, things had changed. It had started with his trip to Charlotte, when Caty had occupied most of his thoughts and entering Harland hadn't made him want to turn around and take off. He'd felt it the other day when Marianne had made pot roast in the middle of the week because it was his favorite. Again when Kyle had grinned up at him with a swipe of grease on his chin while they'd tuned up Matt's motorcycle.

For the first time he could remember, he felt that he belonged here. It didn't take a genius to figure out Caty had something to do with that. More than something, actually.

Everything.

As he pulled up outside Ruthy's, Matt knew he was wearing a goofy grin, but he didn't care. He was having lunch with the one woman who looked at him and saw beyond what he was to who he could be.

Gift in hand, he walked through the door and stopped short. Dressed in a pink waitress uniform with a ruffled apron and handwritten name tag, Caty stood in the back, chatting with two geezers who were openly flirting with her. Then she glanced up and saw Matt. Her delighted smile warmed him right through, and he strolled over to join her.

"Cute outfit," he said, approvingly. "Guess this means lunch is off?"

"Not a bit. Have a seat and I'll be right there." Eyeing the box, she flashed him a curious little girl's look. "Is that for me?"

"Maybe."

Still grinning like an idiot, Matt took a seat by the window. While he waited for Caty, Lisa sidled over with a pitcher of water and a smirk on her face.

"Do you want to tell Marianne or should I?" she asked as she filled his glass.

Ruthy's selections never changed, but he opened the menu to annoy his nosy sister. "Tell her what?"

"About you and Caty."

He faked a blank look, and she smacked his shoulder. "You're terrible! Do you want something to munch on till Caty gets here?"

"A turkey club and sweet tea would be cool. Thanks."

After a quick hug around his shoulders, she flounced away to get his food. He was halfway through his sandwich when Caty handed off her new table to Lisa and joined him.

"I don't have much time," she said, sneaking a pickle off his plate. "Things are crazy, and I'm a little rusty."

He chuckled. "Try some WD-40."

"Very funny. That reminds me, how about supper tonight?"

"With my family?" Not exactly what he had in mind.

"No, at my place." She pointed at the ceiling. "I'm Ruthy's new tenant."

"Is that safe?" he asked. "I thought you were a klutz in the kitchen."

"I'll figure something out."

"You've been busy while I was gone," he said. "Tell me about it."

Her gift was at the end of the table near the window, and while they talked she kept glancing at it. It was entertaining watching her eye the box, trying not to look like she was eyeing the box.

After a few minutes of that, he took pity on her. "Wanna open it?"

That was all the invitation she needed. She slid it over and tore off the paper. He'd had the salesman put it in a

DVD-player box so she wouldn't know right off what it was. Of course, she no longer owned a TV, so she had no use for a DVD player. The look on her face reminded him of the kids when they got clothes for Christmas.

"Thank you. This is really nice."

He chuckled. "Open it."

Excited now, she popped open the end. When she pulled out the leather case, her eyes widened and her mouth dropped into an O. "You didn't."

She slid the computer out and opened the lid. A little melody played, and the screen came to life with an animated sunrise he'd chosen because she loved mornings. She fingered the track pad and gave him the most amazing smile he'd ever seen.

"Matt, thank you."

Grinning, he sipped some of his tea. "You're welcome."

"You really shouldn't have done this," she admonished him. "I know money's pretty tight for you, with the farm situation and all."

He shrugged as if it was no big thing. "I got a good deal."

Sometime next year, he'd actually own the laptop. He wasn't big on credit, but the delighted sparkle in her eyes was worth every extra penny.

"This was pretty expensive," she pressed, patting the burgundy case. "Why did you buy it?"

"'Cause you needed a computer."

"How did you know which one to get?"

He grinned. "Kyle. He used your old one, so I figured he'd know what to get."

"You put some thought into this, then. Why?"

She was obviously trying to make a point, but he was so far behind her she might as well have been at the finish line. Then inspiration struck. "Because."

A grateful expression drifted across her pretty face, making him feel like a hero. "That's good enough for me."

Around three, Caty bolted from the diner with an advance on her first week's pay and that day's tips in an envelope. Her wallet and everything in it had been destroyed in the fire, so this was all she had to work with. It wasn't much, but she managed to get some very basic clothing and a closeout bedding set with matching curtains.

By the time she'd stocked up on generic toiletries and a few groceries, she had five dollars. She was kicking herself for not having already transferred her money to a Harland bank account. Operating from a distant bank was easy when you had an ATM card and a computer. When you didn't, it was impossible. It wasn't the first time she'd lived hand-to-mouth, but she was woefully out of practice.

Without anything to put in it, a wallet had seemed like a waste of money. She tucked her remaining bill into a plastic sandwich bag and stashed it in the jar underneath a batch of Ruthy's latest experimental cookies. A tantalizing combination of crumb cake and butterscotch, they melted in your mouth.

Supper also came compliments of her new boss: fresh salad and roast beef left over from lunch. They were in the small fridge beside take-out cups of sweet tea. Other than that, the icebox was empty. Fortunately, Caty thought with a grin, she now worked in a restaurant.

Once she spread her new things around, she stood in the center of the room to assess her work. The entire apartment was smaller than her Charlotte bedroom, but the splashes of color brightened things up considerably. Satisfied, she showered and put on her only pair of jeans and a blue tank top with a misty rainbow on it. Far from her usual style, she'd bought it because it was the right size and had cost only two dollars.

Then, after waiting all afternoon, she sat down on her bed with her shiny new laptop. Hooking on to the Wi-Fi Ruthy maintained for her customers, Caty logged into her music account and loaded the contents onto the computer. In deference to Matt, she bought some compilation albums from the rock section and created a playlist to store them in. She even added some new songs for herself. In less than five minutes, the speakers were putting out the latest country-rock anthem about taking the curves life throws at you and making them work.

Bobbing her head in time to the catchy tune, she spread out on the floor the patchwork quilt she'd found in the closet. She set out her borrowed dishes picnic-style and got the food out of the fridge. She'd just popped the roast beef into the microwave when someone knocked on the frame of her open door.

Matt stood there with his hands totally full. A Ruthy's Place take-out bag hung from his wrist so he could hold a foil-topped bottle in his hand. In the other was an enormous bouquet of velvety red roses sprinkled with baby's breath.

"Matt, they're beautiful!" Taking them from him, she breathed in their sweet fragrance. "Is this crystal?" she asked, lifting the elegant vase to see it better.

"It was the only one they had that was big enough."

She assessed him with a long look, and he finally cracked a grin. "Thought it was pretty."

"It is. Very."

There was just enough space for the flowers on her tiny counter, and she stepped back to admire the effect. He didn't strike her as the romantic type, which made his gift that much more thoughtful.

Impulsively, she stood on tiptoe and gave him a quick kiss. Still holding the take-out bag, he pulled her close for another, much longer kiss. Somehow, it felt gentle and strong at the same time. The effect was so amazing, she didn't want it to end.

He drew back, eyes twinkling a warm blue as he grinned down at her. "Is that a thank-you?"

"I guess so," she admitted with a smile of her own.

"Then you're welcome." Kissing the tip of her nose, he set the rest of his load next to the sink. "Something smells good."

"You sound surprised," she teased, then added, "I should've told you I don't drink."

"John told me," he replied, handing the bottle to her. "It's sparkling grape juice. Still goes pop when you open it."

"Are we celebrating something?"

Grinning, he took an object out of his shirt pocket and dangled it in front of her. Attached to a shiny MG fob was a set of brand-new keys.

"They came!"

"Just before I left the farm. Excellent timing, huh?"

Recognizing her own words, she laughed. "Very excellent. I opened a bank account this afternoon so they can transfer my money here from Charlotte. As soon as I have some cash, I'll pay you back."

"Don't worry about it."

She almost insisted, then thought better of it. He was being generous, and she didn't want to ruin the gesture. The microwave dinged, and she asked, "Are you hungry?"

"Starving. Ruthy sent this." He opened the bag to show her half a crumb-topped apple pie.

"Awesome! That's my favorite."

While she pulled out the roast beef, he added the pie to

their picnic. She saw him glance over his shoulder before sliding several twenty-dollar bills under the quilt. Sneaky. When she cleaned up later, she'd find them but he'd be long gone so he wouldn't have to accept her thanks in person. Pretending not to notice, she took their food over and switched the music selection.

"You didn't buy those songs for me, did you?" he asked.

"Yeah. I know you don't like country."

"Well, thanks." He unwound the foil from the bottle and worked the cork loose with a satisfying pop. After filling their plastic cups, he stretched out beside her and tapped his cup against hers. "To getting your wheels back."

"Amen to that," she agreed and took a sip. "Mmm, that's good."

Matt tilted the bottle with a grin. "May was a very good year."

"Now I just need my new license, and I'll be all set."

"Wouldn't worry about that," he said between bites. "Everybody around here knows you."

"It's illegal to drive a car without a license."

"You didn't seem to mind that when you were fixing to steal my truck."

She didn't have a good defense for that, so she just laughed along with him.

"I like what you've done in here," he said with approval. "Looks like a flower garden."

"Thanks. Ruthy won't let me pay her, so I offered to spruce it up a little. She said I can refinish the floors and paint, as long as I keep it light and gender neutral."

"Shouldn't take long," he commented with a quick glance around. "Kind of a step down, isn't it?"

An optimist at heart, Caty didn't normally complain about things she couldn't control. But this was Matt, and she knew he wouldn't hold it against her. "Yeah, but I don't have much choice."

He frowned at that. "Don't tell me. The biddies are talking about us shacking up."

"More or less."

"I thought you did what you wanted no matter what other folks thought."

"That was before." Setting her fork down, she got his full attention. She relayed what Ruthy had told her about her father, and his frown darkened to something more sinister.

She cut him off before he could say the foul word forming on his lips. "Don't. I know it's true, but please don't say it."

"I won't, but I'm thinking it. Real loud," he added with venom.

"I can hear you," she teased to ease the murderous look on his face.

"Guess this means you won't be hunting for him."

"Not anytime soon. I wish I'd never found that letter. The fire would have taken care of it, and I could have just gone on the way I was."

"Not knowing the truth?" Matt gave her a skeptical look. "That doesn't sound like you."

He was right, it didn't sound like her. But she was so disgusted by the whole thing, she finally understood why her mother had lied about it all those years.

"That's what I want," she insisted. "I figure other people must know, even though they're too nice to mention it. I'm staying here in Harland, and I'm going to open my own law practice. I can't do anything about the past, but I don't want to give people any reasons to doubt my judgment now."

"Okay, I get it. I don't like it, but I get it."

"I don't like it, either, but I really think it's for the best."

"I'll go along, then," he grumbled. "To make you happy, not 'cause a bunch of clucking hens can't keep their yaps shut."

"Works for me," she said to lighten the mood.

While they traded small talk, she almost asked if he still planned to return to Charlotte. Then she decided the question would make him feel cornered. It was his choice, and she wouldn't dream of trying to influence him. She truly loved this man, and she prayed they might have a future together.

But in the end, it was up to him.

Chapter Thirteen

One Saturday afternoon in late October, they actually knocked off while it was still light. John headed into town for his delayed date with Annie Granger, and Marianne took the kids to see the latest Disney 3-D movie. Caty was working the closing shift at the diner and had begged off seeing Matt so she could go to the Fairmans' for supper. She was exhausted, and he wanted her to relax, so he hid his disappointment and wished her good-night.

The only problem was, it left him completely on his own.

After living alone for so long, coming and going as he pleased, since returning to Harland he'd gotten used to always having someone around. Even Tucker was MIA today, although Matt could hear excited barking coming from the back woodlot. If the crazy Lab brought home another half-dead squirrel, Marianne wouldn't let him back in the house for a month.

Matt ran through the shower and pulled on some sweats he hadn't worn in a while. They just about fell off him, and he had to tighten the laces on the waistband. His farming/fitness routine was a success, he mused, grinning as he rummaged through the fridge. He wasn't all that hungry, so he grabbed an apple and headed back outside.

Every vehicle on the farm was running like a top, and he'd just washed and waxed his truck. His bike didn't need anything, either. So he wandered around, looking at nothing in particular.

The sun was setting, and the blend of red-and-orange streaks in the sky caught his attention. Framed by the show of color, the ancient oak tree's turning leaves made a picture all their own. He didn't know why, but he strolled over and sat down with his back against the rough tree trunk. While he finished his apple, he watched the sun slide bit by bit beneath the horizon, turning the sky over to the harvest moon, glowing more brightly as day gave way to night.

Dad's favorite place, he mused, looking up at the moonlight filtering through the branches. From here, Matt could see hundreds of acres in one direction, woods in another, and the two houses out toward the road. This was his family's history, and against his wishes it had become his responsibility.

Next week was the beginning of November, which meant he had to give his boss an answer on when he was coming back. The thing was, sometime over the last couple months, *when* had become *if.* Matt still wasn't a farmer at heart, but he didn't mind it as much as he once had.

Being in Harland wasn't as suffocating as he remembered, either. Sure, people were nosy, and the interest in his changing relationship with Caty wasn't exactly welcome. But he understood the reason for it. He didn't have the best reputation, and she was one of the town darlings. They were mostly worried about him ruining her, which made him smile.

As if she'd let him.

David the highfalutin lawyer had soured her on taking

risks with men. In a way, he'd done her a favor. His betrayal had made her more cautious, which was fine with Matt. He didn't mind digging in and working a little harder with Caty. She was more than worth it.

When had he decided that? Thinking back, he sifted through the past three months and came up with the answer. It was after he'd returned from Charlotte, when he couldn't get her out of his mind no matter how hard he'd tried. He'd even attempted avoiding her, which had only made him think about her more.

That was a long time ago, he realized, grinning at his own stupidity. How dense could he be? Just thinking about her made Matt happier than he'd ever been in his life. Riding those emotions, he suddenly understood why his father had never remarried. He couldn't imagine himself with anyone but Jan, and he'd preferred being alone to settling for anything less than the love he'd had with her.

That was the kind of love Matt had been searching for all these years. He just hadn't realized it.

There was something about this tree, he thought as he pulled out his phone and dialed his boss's number. Sitting here made him see things differently. Maybe there was a little of Dad left in this spot. Whatever the reason, Matt's tough decision had just gotten a lot easier.

Caty hurried through the door into her tiny apartment and checked the clock on her computer. She'd rushed out to Kenwood to buy something decent for church and had just enough time to de-tag her new clothes and get dressed. It had been a long, challenging week, but she had a lot to be thankful for. She was determined to go thank God in person.

She tucked her pretty ivory blouse into the waistband of her burgundy skirt and zipped everything up. Smiling, she took her splurge out of its box and unwrapped the tissue from around a pair of black suede pumps accented with little velvet bows in the back. She'd bought the exact same pair a few years ago and had been thrilled today to find them at the shoe outlet next to a petite-clothing store.

After slipping them on, she went into the bathroom and pulled her hair into a French twist. Assessing her reflection, she frowned. This really wasn't her look anymore. She took her hair down and pulled it back with a hair band so it fell in loose waves down her back. Much better. Her silver choker glittered in the light, and she grasped it for a dose of encouragement.

Ruthy had told her she could have this room as long as she needed it, which Caty really appreciated. But she wouldn't be a waitress for long. After some serious consideration, she'd decided to use the insurance money to pay off her student loans and bank the rest. She'd let people know she was ready to take on any kind of legal work, from real estate to pet adoption.

With her stellar credit and lawyer's credentials, she could easily borrow enough to rebuild her darling little house. It wouldn't be exactly the same, but it would fill the gaping hole on Oak Street. And the one in her heart.

She would keep believing, Caty vowed, and count her blessings every day. Because, really, the alternative didn't suit her at all.

Someone knocked on the door, and she called out, "Who is it?"

"Sawyer car service."

"What on earth?" she muttered as she hurried to unlock her door. What she saw on the other side rendered her completely speechless.

There stood Matt, wearing the same suit he'd worn to Ethan's funeral. Today, she noticed that his tie exactly matched the color of her new skirt. She couldn't be sure, but she thought he'd even shined his shoes.

After giving her a quick once-over, he grinned. "You look great."

"I used some of the money you left me for some new clothes."

"Money?" he echoed.

"Yes, Matthew." Thanks to the heels, she didn't have to stretch very far to kiss him. "Thank you."

"I really like the way you thank me." Wrapping his arms around her back, he pulled her close. "Missed you."

His voice had a warm, mellow quality that made her go all squishy inside. "I missed you, too. Where are you going dressed so nice?"

"With you."

"But I'm going to church."

"I know." He looked totally calm, but she caught the trace of uncertainty in his eyes.

Baffled, she reminded him, "My license came in the mail yesterday. I told you that."

"I know," he repeated. Tracing the curve of her cheek with his finger, he quietly added, "I want to go with you."

"Don't do this for me," she said, concerned that he was making a big decision for the wrong reason.

"I'm not. I'm doing it for me."

He was looking her straight in the eyes when he said it, and this time she didn't see even a flicker of hesitation.

"What changed your mind?" she asked.

"The night of the fire. I asked God to let you live, and He did."

Astonished, she didn't know what to say. "You prayed for me?"

"Worse. I got on my knees and begged." He didn't look

very happy about it, but that he'd made such a huge gesture to save her touched her deeply.

"Does this mean you've forgiven God?"

"Yeah, I have. Mom was too sick for anyone to save, even Him." Looking down, he took a deep breath and then reconnected with Caty. "I still hate it, but I can live with it."

She remained silent to give him a chance to mull that over. He held her gaze with a steady one of his own. No gray clouded his blue eyes. In them was a calm she'd never seen when he mentioned his mother.

Well-and-truly amazed, she whispered, "You're serious."

"Yeah, I am. Muffin."

Rolling her eyes, she laughed at his latest attempt at a nickname for her. "Try again."

"Puddin'."

"What's with the food names?" she asked as she closed and locked the door.

"I'm starving. I got up late and had to pick between breakfast and shining my shoes."

Ruthy wouldn't open the diner until noon, but her ever-popular Sunday brunch was already in progress. Caty grabbed a fresh blueberry muffin from one of the cooling racks and handed it to him. "Eat fast."

Four bites was all it took, and he managed those while opening her door and starting his truck.

"That's incredible," she commented while they drove to church at the snail's pace speed limit.

"I love blueberry muffins."

Caty made a mental note to ask Ruthy for the recipe. Then again, she thought, considering her own lack of finesse with all things culinary, she'd do better to buy them already made. Matt would probably prefer to enjoy them without risk of food poisoning.

"After I talked to you yesterday, I went out by that old oak tree." He parked the truck, then turned to her. "I sat there a long time, and I think I figured out what all us Sawyers have in common."

"What did you come up with?"

"Love. We love each other, even though we make each other crazy. We also love that farm, because it's just as much a part of our family as any person ever was. That's why we're all killing ourselves to hang on to it."

"Good job," she approved, patting his cheek. "You got it."

"There's one more thing we all love. Even the kids and Tucker."

He'd solved her riddle, so this other thing was something she hadn't considered. "Really? What's that?"

Leaning in, he brushed his lips over hers and smiled. "You."

It was easy to return both the smile and the kiss. "And I love all of you. I just have one question."

"Shoot."

"Does this mean you're staying here in Harland?"

The long, promising kiss he gave her was all the answer she needed.

Matt made it through the entire service without squirming once. He held the hymnal between them, and Caty noticed his voice got stronger with each song. When they came to "Old Rugged Cross," his baritone rang out loud and clear. She recalled it being one of Ethan's favorites, and she could feel him there with his son, bursting with pride.

Matt's presence didn't go unnoticed in the small congregation. Pastor Charles, bless him, didn't single Matt out, but he smiled in their direction several times. There was a warm, generous vibe in the little white church that morning, and Caty suspected Matt was drinking it in the same way she was.

It was a cool morning, so the back doors were closed. One of them creaked as it opened, and Caty glanced back to see who was coming in. She didn't know the man, but he looked vaguely familiar. While she was trying to place him, she noticed the horrified look on Ruthy's face. When the woman's eyes connected with hers, Caty knew who he was.

Brian Jameson.

Her heart jumped into her throat, and she felt her face burning with embarrassment as she faced forward. Ruthy had recognized him instantly. How many other people had, too? Matt reached for her hand, but she yanked it away and shifted as far from him as she could without crushing Lisa.

Sighing, he folded his hands and let them dangle in front of him. When the service was finally over, Caty bolted out the side door without a word to anyone. Matt had the sense to let her go, but he easily caught up with her outside. She couldn't outrun him in her pretty new shoes, but she refused to even look at him.

"Just talk to the man," he said quietly. "He came all the way here from Raleigh to see you."

"How *dare* you," she spat, whirling around to glare up at him for all she was worth. "You knew how I felt, why I felt that way, and you went behind my back to find him. It was my decision, Matthew, not yours."

To her astonishment, he didn't retaliate. Didn't tell her she was being foolish or immature, which even in her state she fully recognized. He didn't say a word, leaving her wide-open to keep on going.

"Is this why you came to pick me up?" she asked. "So I couldn't leave?"

"That would've been pretty clever, but no, I didn't plan it that way." His eyes were locked with hers, and she saw he was telling the truth.

"Why would you do it at church, of all places?" she demanded, sweeping a hand at the crowd of people, who were clearly eavesdropping while trying to look as if they weren't listening.

"Oh, I don't know." Folding his arms, he gave her a look that was something between a scowl and a smile. "I thought it might keep you from making a scene."

"I haven't even started making a scene!" When she heard herself shouting, she took a long breath to cool her temper. "Why is my meeting him so important to you?"

"I'd give anything to talk to my father again," he said in a quiet voice filled with remorse. "I didn't want you to regret never knowing yours."

I wouldn't, she wanted to snarl, but she wasn't sure it was the truth. Brian's unexpected appearance had unnerved her so completely, she felt as if her world had flipped upside down. That seemed to be happening to her a lot lately, and she'd had more than enough of it.

"How on earth did you find him?" she asked.

"Started with the address on that letter he sent you. His folks still live there, and they got me in touch."

"The envelope burned up in the fire," she pointed out.

When Matt just tapped his temple, she fought the overwhelming urge to find a stepladder and strangle him.

"I do *not* want to talk to him now," she seethed, glimpsing him out of the corner of her eye.

"Fine," Matt agreed tersely. "What about me?"

"Don't push it, Sawyer."

With that, she gathered up what was left of her dignity

and stalked away. The fact that no one stopped her to talk told her they all knew perfectly well who their Sunday visitor was. Caty couldn't decide if she was more furious with Brian for being there, with Matt for arranging it, or with herself for being such a horrible coward.

She dreaded the first time someone got up the nerve to ask her about her father. It would be sooner rather than later, she knew. In Harland, this kind of drama wouldn't stay under wraps for long. Half expecting Matt to pull alongside her in his truck and offer her a ride back to the diner, she mentally prepared a scathing reply. When he didn't, she was kind of disappointed.

Of course, if he did happen to show up right now, they'd just resume their pointless argument where they'd left off. She couldn't blame him for staying out of firing range.

Matt knew he'd blown it, big-time.

Angry wasn't the word for how Caty had looked at him. He wasn't sure there even was a word for it, but he wasn't in a hurry to see that expression again anytime soon. His first assessment of her all those weeks ago had been dead-on. She was a real handful.

Then again, he mused with a grin, that was part of her charm.

Right now, Brian Jameson was standing alone beside a tree, watching his daughter all but run away from him. Bracing himself for a difficult conversation, Matt strolled over, hoping he looked friendly and unconcerned.

"Matt Sawyer," he said, offering his hand. "Good to meet you."

With a half smile, Brian shook his hand. "Thanks. I think you're the only person here who feels that way."

"Don't worry about them. They're just nosy."

Motioning toward a secluded picnic table, Matt led

Brian away from the people milling around the church entrance, trying to get a look at him without appearing to gawk. Brian relaxed a little but didn't sit down, so Matt remained standing.

The poor guy looked completely miserable. "I shouldn't have come."

"When we talked, you said you'd think about calling her," Matt pointed out as patiently as he could.

"I know, but I was afraid she'd just hang up on me. This was so much better," he added in a sarcastic tone that instantly reminded Matt of Caty.

"I'm curious about something," Matt began. When Brian nodded, he continued. "Why didn't you go see her when her mother died?"

All the color drained from his face, and the man sank to the bench as if someone had sucker punched him. "Lynn is gone? When? What happened?"

"Caty was nine, and it was a car crash." Feeling like the grim reaper, Matt sat down opposite his guest. "They were in Raleigh at the time, so it must've been in the papers."

"I was traveling for work a lot back then. My parents probably didn't mention it, thinking it would upset me. Even after all that happened, she meant the world to me," he added eagerly, his expression begging for understanding.

"What about your wife?"

He sighed. "Not so much. We divorced just after Caitlin was born."

Matt was dying to know how this seemingly decent man rationalized cheating on his wife and fathering a child with another woman. Unfortunately, it wasn't any of his business.

"You're welcome to come out to the farm for lunch if you want," he said.

"No, I should get going." Taking out his wallet, Brian handed him a business card. "Please tell Caitlin she can call me anytime. If she wants to see me, I'll gladly come back," he added in a shaky voice.

Matt noticed he used her full name. That was probably how he'd thought of her all these years. His little Caitlin, wrapped in a pink blanket, growing up without him. "I'll do that. And I'm sorry if I made a mess of things."

"You didn't," Brian assured him with a sad smile. "I managed that all on my own. But that's not Caitlin's fault, and I'd love to get to know her if she'll let me. She's beautiful, isn't she?"

"Yeah, she is. Inside and out."

Pride filled Brian's green eyes, and they glinted with tears. "I've missed so much with her. I'd hate to miss any more."

"Give her time to think it through. She'll come around."

As Brian walked toward his car, Matt hoped he was right. The first time around, Caty had had nothing to do with locking her father out of her life. This time, she had a choice.

Brian was her only family. If she couldn't forgive him, Matt worried that someday Brian would be gone and it would be too late. From painful personal experience, Matt knew that kind of guilt stayed with you forever.

After a while you learned how to carry it around, but it never went away.

By noon, Caty's little apartment had begun to feel claustrophobic. Brooding had never suited her, and she was dying to go somewhere else. Ordinarily, she'd be at the farm helping with lunch, but she wasn't ready to face Matt. With no particular plans, she went out to her car and put the top down. Maybe a long drive would help clear her mind, and she'd know what to do about the two incredibly aggravating men in her life.

Before long, the beautiful day lifted her spirits, even though her mind was still twisted in knots. Raised with impeccable Southern manners, she knew she'd been unconscionably rude to Brian. He'd driven so far—seeing her must have been very important to him. She should have at least spoken to him, given him a chance to explain.

Life and law school had taught her there were at least two sides to every story. She'd judged him without ever hearing his side, and that was wrong. Not as wrong as what he'd done all those years ago, but wrong all the same.

The road curved to the left, and she followed it to the gates of the cemetery. It had been a while since she'd visited her mother's and grandparents' graves. Going there always made her feel better, so she turned into the gravel driveway. She crested a small hill and paused, unable to believe her eyes.

There, beside her mother's stone with a huge bouquet of red roses in his hands, stood Brian Jameson. She heard a few murmurs of his voice on the breeze, then nothing. Tears were rolling down his cheeks, and she couldn't help feeling sorry for him.

If he'd been a stranger, she would have empathized with his loss. God knew she'd experienced enough of it to relate to how he was feeling. A sudden realization hit her, knotting her thoughts even tighter.

Until today, he hadn't known her mother had died.

All these years, he'd respected her wishes and stayed away. Matt's phone call must have been a shock, but Brian had climbed in his car and driven to meet his daughter with no guarantee of the outcome. He must have known she might reject him. Why would he take such a risk?

The answer was obvious: he loved her. The little girl

who still lived inside her skipped up with the idea that he wanted to get to know her. Then Caty's logical grown-up mind took over. It simply couldn't balance that possibility against the adultery thing.

Tired and confused, she drove past the touching scene and back out to the highway. When she realized she was headed for Ryker's Ridge, her mind looped back to Matt.

Her temper began simmering again, and this time she let it bubble. He'd deliberately gone against her wishes, deciding he knew what was best for her. Why? she fumed, still too furious to remember his explanation.

Asphalt gave way to dirt, and she followed the winding road up into the hills. At the spot where they'd enjoyed that intimate, soul-baring conversation, she got out and walked over to the rock where she'd been sitting when he'd opened his heart to her and she'd been crazy enough to walk in. A gentle breeze touched her cheek, and his sorrowful voice echoed in her mind.

I'd give anything to talk to my father again. I didn't want you to regret never knowing yours.

Understanding washed over her, and some of her anger dissipated. Matt had gone over the line contacting Brian that way, but this time it wasn't because he was arrogant and wanted to be right. He'd done it for her. Just as he'd fixed her roof and replaced her locks. The same way he'd taken the first steps that had brought the two of them together. And climbed into a raging fire, then begged God to spare her life.

For all his faults, Matt loved her. He'd proven it time and again, so she knew it was for real. Brian's actions today clearly said he loved her, too. Maybe, if she gave him a chance, they could overcome the past and build some kind of relationship. But first she'd have to forgive him. She wasn't sure she could.

Where did that leave her? she wondered as she drove back into town. With a tangled mess and no clear solution. She was accustomed to examining issues from all angles to differentiate right from wrong. The trouble was, when it came to people, things weren't quite so black-and-white.

There was a lot of gray in the world, she'd discovered over the past few months. She really hated gray.

Chapter Fourteen

Even though he was dog tired, Matt lay in his bed, staring at the ceiling. He'd gone over and over everything in his mind, wondering if he could have handled the situation with Brian differently. The answer was yes, but he still thought he'd done the right thing. He just had to give Caty a chance to realize that, and things would be good between them.

It had occurred to him that she might never forgive him. He'd invaded her very private ground, and he didn't blame her for being angry with him. Because it was still uncomfortable, he was hesitant to formally ask God for help with the sweet, headstrong woman he'd so unexpectedly fallen in love with. Around one, though, he finally relented.

"Please help her forgive me. I was just trying to help."

There was no flash of lightning or boom of thunder to tell him "message received." Sighing, he rolled over and tried to put it out of his mind. Stubborn as she was, it wouldn't surprise him if Caty's turnaround took a while.

Patience wasn't his strong point, but it wasn't as if he had much choice. He'd gone over the line, and it was up to her to forgive him. Or not. He really hated not being able to fix things, but in this case, he just didn't know how.

Machinery, no problem. He grabbed hold of it, tearing it apart until he'd figured out what was wrong. He couldn't do that with emotions. That's why he'd always steered far clear of them.

Until Caty. She had a knack for making him feel things. Happiness. Frustration. Blind, desperate fear. It was the last that had forced him back to the path his father had always wanted him to follow. No matter what happened, Matt would always be grateful to Caty for making it happen. He and God had a rocky history, but it was good to know God was still on his side.

Just after Matt drifted off, he heard a faint tapping on his window. Thinking it was a tree branch, he ignored it and tried to get back to sleep. When he heard it a few more times, he groaned and hauled himself out of bed to snap off the irritating branch.

At the window, he realized there was no breeze blowing through the tree.

"Hey, there."

Looking down, he saw Caty standing below him with a handful of gravel. Despite the nasty day he'd ground his way through, he felt a grin pop up all on its own. "Hey, yourself. What're you doing here?"

She dropped the gravel and then looked back up at him. "I need to talk to you, but I didn't want to wake everyone else up knocking on the door."

Her phrasing and apologetic tone made him smile even more. She *needed* to talk to him, and she didn't sound mad about it. Maybe, just maybe, that meant he was off the hook.

"It's unlocked, y'know."

"I'm a lawyer," she reminded him curtly. "I don't just walk into people's houses uninvited."

"Why didn't you call my cell?"

"I did, but it went straight to voice mail. You must have forgotten to charge it."

He didn't doubt that. Since the fire, he'd had a lot on his mind.

"I think we've got this backwards," he teased, balancing his arms across the sill. "I'm supposed to be the one sneaking in to see you in the middle of the night."

She laughed quietly. "Grandpa would've chased you off with a seat full of buckshot."

"That sounds painful."

"This conversation is painful," she shot back. "Will you let me in or not?"

"Sure. Meet you downstairs."

Dressed in sweats and a ratty T-shirt, he padded downstairs in his bare feet. When he opened the kitchen door, he wasn't sure what to do next. He wanted to take her in his arms, apologize for stepping in where he never should have been in the first place. He really wanted to kiss her and hear her say she forgave him. He wanted to tell her again that he loved her. The words were new for him, but he liked the way they made him feel.

But she made no move to come in, and the stern expression on her face made him glad there was a screen door between them.

"You sent Brian out to the cemetery, didn't you?" she demanded.

He shrugged, hoping he looked unconcerned. "I figured you might go there."

"Why did he go?"

"He thought your mom was still alive. You should've seen his reaction when I told her she died twenty years ago. He just about collapsed."

"He brought her roses," she snapped.

Matt decided he'd had enough of this lethal back-and-forth. He'd never won an argument with her, and this wasn't likely to be his first victory. He knew if he went at her directly, she'd cut him off and quit listening. So he went with humor.

"Last I knew, that wasn't a crime in North Carolina."

A smile tugged at the corner of her mouth before she could straighten it into a disapproving line. "If that's your best defense, I'm leaving."

She turned to go, but he pushed the door open and caught her hand just before she left the porch. "Don't go. I just like messing with you."

"You're very good at it," she huffed, not looking at him.

"I have two sisters." Reeling her in for a kiss, he rubbed noses with her. "I've had lots of practice."

In the moonlight, he saw the warmth come back into those amazing green eyes. "I don't even want to think about all the things you've had practice with."

"Good plan."

He flashed a grin that finally made her laugh. "You're really, really bad, you know that?"

"Yeah, and I'm all yours."

"How lucky am I?" she retorted.

"Very."

She studied him for what felt like a long time, and he wondered for the millionth time what was going on in that quick mind of hers. Finally, she seemed to decide something and smiled up at him. "Thank you for bringing my father back to me, Matthew."

"You're welcome."

Epilogue

It was Christmas Eve.

This year, despite Ethan's absence, Marianne had decided to throw her usual celebration after church. Caty lost count of the guests milling around the house, mingling and chatting, some singing carols near the gigantic tree in the living room. Kyle and Emily had dragged the rest of the family from one end of the woodlot to the other before settling on a twelve-foot spruce. The boughs held hundreds of lights and treasured ornaments, and the antique crystal star on top grazed the living room ceiling.

There were so many people that the crowd spilled out onto the porches, where decorated pine trees and swags of lighted garland mimicked the inside decor. Caty was on the much quieter back porch, waiting for her father. He didn't know many people in Harland, and she didn't want him walking into a sea of less-than-friendly strangers.

Her father.

Even though they'd visited back and forth a few times, the idea of it still gave her a chill. A good one, because she couldn't believe that after all these years, she was getting to know the man who'd been absent from her life but had never forgotten his little girl.

When he parked his car on the side of the driveway, she went out to meet him.

"Merry Christmas!" she said, giving him a quick hug. "How was your trip?"

"Fine." He gave her the same warm smile she'd seen in that old picture. "Have I missed anything?"

"No. Marianne's got enough food for an army."

She turned to go, but he called her back. "I have something for you."

He reached in his car to pop the trunk and walked around to open it. Inside were stacks of presents, all wrapped differently.

"Wow," she commented. "It must have taken you hours to buy and wrap all those."

"It wasn't that much, really." Looking hesitant, he cleared his throat. "They're for you."

"For me?" she echoed, totally stumped. "Why so many?"

"Every year at Christmas, I bought something for you. I missed you every day, but it was worst at Christmas. Getting you a gift made me feel a little closer to you." Digging through, he pulled out a package wrapped in faded paper and handed it to her. "This was for your first Christmas."

Looking at the tag, Caty saw the year written beside her name. Then she looked at the pile in his trunk, and tears welled in her eyes. "You bought me a present every year?"

"The boxes got smaller as you got older," he explained in a rush, as if he expected her to cut him off. "Jewelry, watches, things like that. I tried to get things I thought a young lady would enjoy."

"You kept them all this time?" she choked out around the lump in her throat.

"I prayed we'd meet someday and I'd have a chance to give them to you."

She stared up at him in disbelief. "You prayed about meeting me?"

He reached out and took her free hand. "Caitlin, when I met your mom, I was a selfish, miserable young man. She showed me what I was missing, and I'll always be grateful to her for that." His expression grew thoughtful. "When you were born, something changed inside me. I'd gotten away from my faith, and I think God saw enough good in me to bring me back. Since then, I've done my best to live right."

That did it. Tears streaming down her cheeks, Caty opened the package to find a slightly flattened pink bunny staring out at her from its tissue-paper nest. She pulled it out and smoothed the fur, marveling at the love he'd shown her, even when she didn't know who he was.

Gazing up at the man she'd longed for her entire life, she could think of only one thing to say. "Thank you." Gathering her courage, she swallowed hard. "Dad."

His own eyes brimming over, her father opened his arms, and she went into them, cuddling that precious stuffed animal between them.

It was like the sappy final scene from an old-fashioned Christmas movie. And it felt absolutely wonderful.

"I love Christmas Eve," John announced, catching Caty for a quick peck on the cheek.

Laughing, she pointed across the living room to the archway that led into the kitchen. "Mistletoe's over there."

"You're a lawyer. Sue me." He gave her his blinding country-boy grin and sauntered off to continue spreading his own special brand of Christmas cheer.

On her way into the kitchen, Caty stopped to chat with several of the hundred or so guests milling around the main floor of the Sawyers' farmhouse. "Marianne, you've outdone yourself again this year," Caty complimented her with a hug. "Everyone's having a great time."

Focused on the tray of small quiches she was preparing, Marianne smiled. "They seem to be. I wasn't sure we should do it, but Matt said Dad would want us to. It was a very un-Matt-like thing to say."

"People change," Caty replied.

"You had a little something to do with that." Pulling on candy-cane oven mitts, Marianne slid a tray of quiches from the oven and replaced them with uncooked ones. "He didn't come that far on his own."

Marianne wasn't the first person to say something like that. As Caty arranged the yummy treats on a platter, she allowed herself a smile. She might have made Matt's life a little better, but he'd helped her find things she'd thought she'd lost forever.

He'd taught her to trust, in herself and others. But most important, he'd taught her to love without fear of losing. Strong and solid as the farm he'd fought to save, he'd shown her that some things were worth the risk.

"Now that your stubborn big brother's settled," she began, "you could be next."

Marianne shook her head. "I've sworn off men, remember?"

"Oh, come on." Caty laughed. "There are still some good ones around."

"Maybe," Marianne commented in a tone that said she didn't really believe that. "Unfortunately, my ex-husband taught me they're just not worth the trouble they cause."

In the interest of keeping peace on Christmas Eve, Caty decided it was best to let the subject drop. "So, what do you and the kids have planned for Christmas vacation?"

Glancing around, Marianne whispered, "Now that Emily's old enough, I'm taking them to Charlotte for a few days. One of the hotels downtown has a package deal with the theater showing that kids' Broadway musical. I also managed to get day passes for the new indoor amusement park. It's one of their Christmas presents."

"From that smile, I'd say you're as psyched about it as they're going to be."

"It's been tough around here. It'll be nice to get away for a few days."

As Marianne left to take the quiches into the living room, Matt came up behind Caty, dropping his head over her shoulder to give her a hug.

"Was my little brother bugging you earlier?" he murmured in her ear.

"No more than usual." She tilted her head to look back at him. "Congratulations, by the way. Rededicating yourself as a Christian on Christmas Eve is fabulous."

"Caused quite a stir, didn't we?"

"Oh, you loved it. Ruthy was so proud of you, I thought she was gonna cry."

"How 'bout you?" he asked, taking her hand to lead her back to the festivities. "Were you proud of me?"

"And then some. Which reminds me, how did the farm audit go?"

"Well, we're not exactly millionaires, but we're treading water." He popped a cream puff in his mouth and just about swallowed it whole. "After next year's harvest, I might even be able to pay myself."

"That's awesome news! Congratulations."

"Couldn't have done it without you."

"Or your family," she added. "We all make a good team."

"Your dad looks like he's enjoying himself."

They glanced toward the couch where Brian sat with

Emily on one knee, listening patiently while she talked his ear off.

"I have a bunch of cousins scattered around, but he never had any more children," Caty told him. "He's such a nice man, it's really sad."

"He's got you now," Matt reminded her. "That's enough for any guy to manage."

"So funny."

Rolling her eyes, Caty was surprised when he stopped under the mistletoe. Because they didn't want any grief from anyone, they'd kept their kisses private. This one would be in full view of half the town. Interpreting that as progress, she gladly accepted his quick kiss and moved to keep walking.

When he tugged her to a stop, she turned with a confused look. "What?"

Settling his arms around her waist, he smiled down at her. "I wanted to give you my present tonight. It's kind of a two-parter."

Intrigued by the twinkle in his eyes, she waited for him to go on.

"I've spent a lot of years running away from things." He was frowning now, but the twinkle was still there so she let him talk. "I didn't know it at the time, but now I see it for what it was." His expression softened into a lazy smile, and he chuckled. "No matter how hard I tried, I couldn't outrun you. You wouldn't chase after me, but you wouldn't let me go, either."

"Yeah, I'm stubborn like that."

"I'm glad you are." Warmth flooded his eyes, washing over her from head to toe. "I love you, Caty."

It was the first time he'd said it so directly, and in full hearing of their guests, no less. Stunned beyond belief, she actually had to remind herself to breathe. She stared up at him, this maddening man who'd pulled her in, only to push her away. And then, when she'd needed him most, he'd risked his life to save her. She understood how much it meant to him to say those words. Because he took them so seriously, she knew he felt them with all his heart.

When she found her voice, she beamed up at him. "I love you, too, Matthew."

Gathering her in his arms, he gave her another, much longer kiss as her feet left the ground and he spun her around under the mistletoe.

When he set her down, the mischief lighting his eyes warned her to brace herself for part two.

"I finally thought of a nickname for you."

"Great," she sighed. "Let's hear it."

He reached above the doorway for something sitting on the wide casing. Bringing it down, he fiddled with it for a second and then held it out. Nestled in a blue velvet box was an antique engagement ring. Gold and diamonds surrounded by dainty filigree, it was the most beautiful piece of jewelry she'd ever seen.

Grinning, he picked up her left hand and slid it onto her finger. "How 'bout Mrs. Sawyer?"

For several moments, all she could do was admire that stunning ring. It could be hers, along with the man cradling her hand so gently in his. Somehow, she tore her eyes away and looked up at him. Matt was offering her everything she'd ever wanted, and all she had to do was reach out and take it.

When she finally found her voice, she answered the most important question of her life with one simple word.

"Perfect."

* * * * *

If you enjoyed Mia Ross's book, be sure to check out the other books this month from Love Inspired!

Dear Reader,

Hometown Family is my debut for Love Inspired, and I hope you enjoyed Matt and Caty's story. So often, we get caught up in the past and forget that we have the power to make tomorrow better than today. To do that, we have to learn to forgive and follow the path God has in mind for each of us. Sometimes the trail is a little overgrown, but if we look carefully it's there.

The message of this book is a simple one: if you can believe, all things are possible. Whether it's belief in Him, someone else or ourselves, that faith helps even out the bumps in the road and make our lives all they were meant to be.

If you'd like to stop by for a visit, you'll find me online at www.miaross.com. While you're there, send me an email. I'd love to hear from you!

Mia Ross

Questions for Discussion

1. Caty knows that for Matt and her to have a future, he needs to embrace God. It's a difficult thing for him because it requires him to have a change of heart. Do you think such a fundamental change is possible?

2. One of the themes in this story is forgiveness. Have you ever been reluctant to forgive someone? How did your faith help you overcome that reluctance?

3. With patience and persistence, Caty helps Matt understand that God wasn't responsible for his mother's death. This allows him to forgive God and allow Him back into his life. Has something similar ever happened to you?

4. Ruth Benton is a pragmatic but compassionate Christian who strives to make life better for those around her. Do you know anyone like her? Or are you that rock for someone else?

5. After losing her job, Caty suffers from an almost paralyzing fear of failing again. Matt tells her she'll get past it, and eventually she does. Can you think of a time when you faced and conquered your own fear?

6. When Matt discovers the farm is bankrupt, his first instinct is to sell the land and get on with his life. Later, he realizes he'd be letting his entire family down, and he couldn't live with himself. Have you encountered situations like this in your own life? If so, how did you handle them?

7. The night of the fire, Matt humbles himself and begs God to save Caty's life. This is a turning point for him, both spiritually and with Caty. Have similar circumstances in your own life changed your perspective on what's truly important to you?

8. Caty and Matt are slow to trust each other. When does Caty start to trust Matt and why? When does Matt start to trust Caty and why?

9. Matt neglected his family for years and had to make some serious concessions to strengthen those bonds. Why did it take him so long? Do you have relationships in need of rebuilding?

10. *If you can believe, all things are possible.* This phrase shows up throughout the book and is important to both Caty and Matt. What does it mean to each of them?

11. Because of her earlier impressions of Matt, Caty doesn't like him at first. Then she learns more about him and what a good heart he has. Have you ever known anyone like that?

12. Caty was raised believing her father abandoned her. Just when she starts thinking about contacting him, she discovers he was married and had an affair with her mother. He begs Caty to let him prove he's a different man now. Do you think people are capable of such radical change?

INSPIRATIONAL

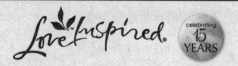

celebrating
15
YEARS

COMING NEXT MONTH
AVAILABLE MAY 29, 2012

THE PROMISE OF HOME
Mirror Lake
Kathryn Springer

A DREAM OF HIS OWN
Dreams Come True
Gail Gaymer Martin

HEALING THE DOCTOR'S HEART
Home to Hartley Creek
Carolyne Aarsen

THE NANNY'S TWIN BLESSINGS
Email Order Brides
Deb Kastner

THE FOREST RANGER'S CHILD
Leigh Bale

ALASKAN HEARTS
Teri Wilson

REQUEST YOUR FREE BOOKS!

2 FREE INSPIRATIONAL NOVELS
PLUS 2
FREE
MYSTERY GIFTS

Love Inspired®

YES! Please send me 2 FREE Love Inspired® novels and my 2 FREE mystery gifts (gifts are worth about $10). After receiving them, if I don't wish to receive any more books, I can return the shipping statement marked "cancel." If I don't cancel, I will receive 6 brand-new novels every month and be billed just $4.49 per book in the U.S. or $4.99 per book in Canada. That's a saving of at least 22% off the cover price. It's quite a bargain! Shipping and handling is just 50¢ per book in the U.S. and 75¢ per book in Canada.* I understand that accepting the 2 free books and gifts places me under no obligation to buy anything. I can always return a shipment and cancel at any time. Even if I never buy another book, the two free books and gifts are mine to keep forever.

105/305 IDN FEGR

Name	(PLEASE PRINT)	
Address		Apt. #
City	State/Prov.	Zip/Postal Code

Signature (if under 18, a parent or guardian must sign)

Mail to the Reader Service:
IN U.S.A.: P.O. Box 1867, Buffalo, NY 14240-1867
IN CANADA: P.O. Box 609, Fort Erie, Ontario L2A 5X3

Not valid for current subscribers to Love Inspired books.

**Are you a subscriber to Love Inspired books
and want to receive the larger-print edition?
Call 1-800-873-8635 or visit www.ReaderService.com.**

* Terms and prices subject to change without notice. Prices do not include applicable taxes. Sales tax applicable in N.Y. Canadian residents will be charged applicable taxes. Offer not valid in Quebec. This offer is limited to one order per household. All orders subject to credit approval. Credit or debit balances in a customer's account(s) may be offset by any other outstanding balance owed by or to the customer. Please allow 4 to 6 weeks for delivery. Offer available while quantities last.

Your Privacy—The Reader Service is committed to protecting your privacy. Our Privacy Policy is available online at www.ReaderService.com or upon request from the Reader Service.

We make a portion of our mailing list available to reputable third parties that offer products we believe may interest you. If you prefer that we not exchange your name with third parties, or if you wish to clarify or modify your communication preferences, please visit us at www.ReaderService.com/consumerschoice or write to us at Reader Service Preference Service, P.O. Box 9062, Buffalo, NY 14269. Include your complete name and address.

celebrating
15 YEARS

Get swept away with author

Carolyne Aarsen

Saving lives is what E.R. nurse Shannon Deacon excels at.
It also distracts her from painful romantic memories and
the fact that her ex-fiancé's brother, Dr. Ben Brouwer, just
moved in next door. She doesn't want anything to do with
him, but Ben is also hurting from a failed marriage…and
two determined matchmakers think Ben and Shannon can
help each other heal. Will they take a second chance at love?

Healing the Doctor's Heart

Home to
Hartley Creek

Available June 2012 wherever books are sold.

Love Inspired HISTORICAL

celebrating
15
YEARS

Author
WINNIE GRIGGS

brings you another story from

Irish Brides

For two months, Nora Murphy cared for an abandoned infant she found while on her voyage from Ireland to Boston. Now settled in Faith Glen, Nora tells herself she's happy with little Grace and a good job as housekeeper to Sheriff Cameron Long. A traumatic childhood closed Cam off to any dreams of family life. Yet somehow his lovely housekeeper and her child have opened his heart again. When the unthinkable occurs, it will take all their faith to reach a new future together.

A Baby Between Them

Available June 2012 wherever books are sold.